The HEARTland— that place between the coasts where real people live. They work and play, laugh and cry, meet and fall in love. If they stumble and fall, they pick themselves up again and continue to fight the good fight. God and family always come first, friends a close second. They love their country.

You know these people. They are always in the middle of things, the heart and soul of their families and communities. They give their all for those they love. Their beliefs are unshakable. You want them to win. You want the best for them. The only thing you don't want is to be their enemy …

In my fourth HEARTland ROMANCE, ***ON THE EDGE***, you will meet DIA Agent Kendra Allen and ex-Special Forces Major Jared Hall. Kris and Matt discuss them in ***PROMISES KEPT:***

"Kendra is—fragile…emotionally…I just don't want her hurt," Kris explains to Matt. "She's been through a lot. And like someone else I know, she's never learned to deal with it. She handles it by living too close to the edge."

"If that's the case," Matt replies, "then there's no one better than Jared to catch her should she fall."

My fifth HEARTland ROMANCE will be available in the near future at www.lulu.com. You will meet Terri Parker and Michael Braden in ***ON THE EDGE.*** Look for their story, ***BEYOND THE SUNRISE,*** coming soon.

I hope you enjoy these characters as much as I have enjoyed creating them. I wish you FAITH, HOPE & LOVE. May God Bless.

Eva O'Connor

HEARTland Series Book 4:

ON THE EDGE

by

Eva O'Connor

Lulu.com

HEARTland Series Book 4: ON THE EDGE

by Eva O'Connor

Copyright © November 2008 by Eva O'Connor

ISBN: 978-0-578-00194-4

Cover Photograph by the Author

The Lord is on my side; I will not fear.
What can man do unto me?
Psalm 118:6

To all those in our military and intelligence service who live on the edge
in order to keep the rest of us safe.
May they find Peace.

CHAPTER ONE

Win...

Lose...

Jared Hall fought down the feeling of unease and lowered his binoculars. For the first time since starting *Extreme Expeditions*, the sixth sense that had once meant his survival had skulked up to tap him on the shoulder.

...or draw.

He stood on an outcropping of rock and surveyed the campsite below, striving to regain his equilibrium. The next two weeks promised to be interminable. One day into the expedition and the group of female executives, attorneys, and business owners had already tried his patience.

Today was at best a draw. He thought briefly of his days in Special Forces, and then remembered why he had left. A definite *lose*.

He sighed. Glorified babysitter to a group of pampered women who saw themselves as *Xena*, Warrior Princesses, was a role he had willingly chosen. He had no reason to complain.

Oh, these women were attractive enough. Some were outright beautiful. Most had the ability to bore him to tears. His eyes swept the group, looking for the one who didn't fit in. He found her as he expected, apart from the rest. As if she felt his gaze, she raised her head to look in his direction.

Kendra Allen. What was her story? She did not seem to be into sharing as the others were. He'd heard the encapsulated life stories of most of the women over the course of the afternoon and expected to hear a lot more in the days to come. Bonding was a big part of the routine. Kendra had not spoken. He knew. Her husky voice had struck a chord the moment she introduced herself. She had enrolled at the last moment when a previous member of the group had been diagnosed with hepatitis.

Jared stayed in place until the western sky turned a deep purple with streaks of coral, then made his way toward the tent he shared with his fellow team leader. He fought down the urge to speak to Kendra Allen. He wanted to hear her voice again, but had no other reason for singling her out.

"Mr. Hall?" As if his thoughts had somehow conjured her up, he turned at the sound of Kendra's voice.

"May I help you?" He kept his voice formal, and too late, realized that a frown creased his brow.

She studied him for a moment, as if uncertain whether to proceed.

"I saw you up above, as if you were on look out. Are you--maybe expecting trouble?"

"Trouble?" He took time to consider her inquiry. *What would prompt a question like that?* "No. Nothing more than the usual. Who will be the first to get seriously injured? Who forgets, or refuses, to wear a hat or sunscreen. Extreme adventurers, especially ones like these, can be a challenge."

A corner of her mouth quirked. "I quite agree. But don't worry. I wouldn't dare tell anyone the degree of contempt in which you hold us."

"Miss Allen--" he broke off. Tried again. "Not *contempt*, exactly."

She grinned. "Maybe not all the time. But you couldn't quite conceal it when Teri broke her fingernail."

"Yeah, well, she made more noise than SueAnn did when she twisted her ankle."

"She's going to be okay, by the way. I just checked on her a few minutes ago."

Jared raised a brow. "SueAnn or Teri?"

Kendra laughed as he had hoped, sending an answering response along his nerve endings.

"SueAnn, of course. Unless we can come up with superglue, there's no hope for Teri." She rolled her eyes.

"And you're an expert? About SueAnn, that is." He noticed that her fingernails were short, neatly rounded, and natural in color.

She shrugged. "A few Red Cross courses and some EMS training. Nothing like you, but I can help out in a pinch."

"That's good to know. Of course, if SueAnn can't keep up the pace in the morning, we'll have to call in a chopper to take her out."

"She knows. My money's on her. She doesn't want that to happen."

"Could it be that maybe she is hiding her pain, hoping to fool us into thinking she can go on?"

9

It was Kendra's turn to raise a brow. "And would you blame her? She is fully aware of your attitude and doesn't intend to justify it."

"The only way she can justify it is to try to do something that will result in further injuries. Do me a favor and see if you can get that through to her."

Kendra gave a smart salute. "Aye, aye, Major. Will do." She turned away from him.

"Kendra?"

She glanced back.

"The name is Jared."

"Aye, Major."

He shrugged. "Suit yourself, Ms. Allen." He ducked into the tent, then turned to watch through the mesh screen as she took a few steps, then stopped to take a careful look around the darkening glade. After a moment she continued across it to the tent she shared with SueAnn.

What made her so nervous? Jared wondered. She was by far in the best physical shape of any of the attendees. She had more than proven herself today; had in fact probably saved SueAnn from serious injury when she slipped.

It did happen occasionally, Jared reflected, that a serious athlete joined the program. The problem this time was that Kendra Allen didn't seem to need to prove anything to herself or anyone else. She didn't fit the usual profile of *faux* extreme adventurer.

Kendra slipped into her tent and untied her bedroll, being as quiet as possible in order not to disturb SueAnn. She felt edgy and restless and Jared Hall had in no way reassured her. It wasn't his fault that he didn't know why she expected trouble; that she feared she had been followed since cutting short her last mission in Germany. She was having second thoughts now that she realized she might be endangering innocent people, especially in an environment as challenging as this.

In fact, what had really caused SueAnn to lose her footing this afternoon?

"Would you care to tell me why you're so uptight?" Jared Hall dropped down on the rock beside Kendra.

She glanced at him. It was now well past midnight and she sat alone on the outskirts of the camp, having abandoned any attempt to sleep.

"Shouldn't you be sleeping?" she asked. "Tomorrow promises to be a challenge. Your words, I believe."

"I should," he agreed. "And so should you. What kind of trouble are *you* expecting?" She felt him studying her as he waited for an answer.

She stretched her arms over her head, trying to work the tension out of her muscles.

"I shouldn't have come," she said. "I realize now that I may be putting other people in danger."

She felt Jared tense beside her.

"Danger?"

She drew up a knee to clasp her hands around it. "I'm really sorry. I needed to disappear for a couple of weeks and this seemed the ideal solution. Obviously, I didn't think it through."

"Ideal?" Jared snorted. "You could spend a couple of weeks at a posh resort, sipping margaritas on the beach, for a lot less than this cost."

"That's not exactly my scene. Besides, resorts are too visible."

"What? Someone is looking for you?"

"Isn't that the usual reason for wanting to disappear?"

"You think someone will come here looking for you? *With what intent?*"

"Look, maybe I'm overreacting," Kendra said, moving to stand up.

Jared caught her hand, pulled her back down. Released her quickly as he felt a tingle of awareness where their skin touched.

"No, you don't. We've come this far. I don't want any nasty surprises for any of us. I take my responsibilities seriously and these women have trusted me with their lives."

She looked at him. Sighed. "If you call in the chopper for SueAnn tomorrow, I'll leave with her."

"That might work for you, but how will these nameless pursuers know you're gone? What will keep them from coming for you anyway, thus endangering everyone else?"

Kendra swallowed. "I've really screwed up this time, haven't I?"

"You tell me. What is this all about? Why would someone be looking for you?"

She sighed. "I'm in industrial espionage."

"Stealing? Selling?" Jared grated.

"Neither. I find the people who steal and sell. I work for—well, let's just say that I'm hired out. When a job is over I disappear for awhile, then when things die down, I'm reassigned."

"So what went wrong this time?"

"It's almost inevitable that sooner or later you will run into someone you've worked with before."

"That could be true of any job."

"Yes, but when someone disappears as abruptly as I do a couple of times, someone is bound to put two and two together and come up with a very suspicious four."

"And that happened this time?"

"Maybe."

Jared got to his feet. "Sorry, sweetheart. Unless you can do better than that, I think I'll try and get some sleep."

Kendra glanced up at him. "Fine with me. I don't remember asking for your help."

"You didn't. I was a troubleshooter for too long."

She nodded. "Special Forces."

He squinted down at her in the moonlight. "Did I tell you that?"

"You didn't have to." She stood. "There may be more than one Jared Hall. But when I called you Major and you didn't flinch, I figured you were *the* Major Jared Hall."

"And what exactly does *the* Major Jared Hall mean? How could you possibly have heard of me?"

She met his eyes. "I'm sure you don't remember, Major, but you've gotten me out of trouble before."

His eyes widened and she could almost hear his mind working. It took only seconds.

"Kuwait. *At the beginning of the Gulf War.*"

"Right in one, Major."

"And you didn't learn anything of value from that experience?"

Kendra heard the sarcasm in his voice. She raised her head, chin tilted.

"On the contrary. I learned how desperately this country needs people skilled in averting military espionage. I changed my focus slightly."

"Meaning what?"

"Since then I've mostly penetrated military installations, weapons manufacturers, and the like."

"On assignment?"

She nodded.

"Which means there's already suspicion that something underhanded is taking place?"

"You got it."

"And this last assignment? Something happened that concerned you, made you feel vulnerable?" Again, Kendra felt him studying her.

"There were a couple of guys who were suspicious from the beginning. I had excellent faked credentials, but one of them had connections at a place where I was supposed to have worked. He had me checked out. I was able to get most of the evidence I needed before I had to leave rather suddenly, and try to disappear. I didn't get enough, but they don't know that."

"Does anyone have any reason to think you would sign up for an *Extreme Expeditions* course?"

"I don't know. But in this case, they turned out to be better than I was. That doesn't do much to reassure me."

"That doesn't happen often, I gather."

"What doesn't happen often?" Kendra asked in confusion.

"That someone turns out to be better than you."

"What are you trying to say, Major?"

"I'll bet you intimidate every man you work with." He raked a hand through his hair.

She nodded. "About ninety-nine percent of them."

"I can believe that. You sure intimidate me."

Her lips parted as she stared at him. She drew in her breath slowly. "That doesn't do much to reassure me, Major," she said, wetting her lips.

"It wasn't meant to." He raised his head to stare up at the stars for a moment. "As for your problem, I don't know what advice to offer. Tomorrow night we share a camp with another group that crosses our path. After that, I would think you can relax."

Kendra didn't look at him. "Thanks for trying, Major, and caring enough to ask. I'm sorry I'm keeping you awake."

He put a hand on her arm, dropped it quickly. "You need some sleep yourself. I know I didn't say it, but you were great today. Thanks for all the help with SueAnn."

After a moment Kendra forced herself to relax and fell in step with him as they walked back toward the camp. "By the way," she baited him, "when does the hard part start?"

His reply was a deep chuckle that warmed Kendra all the way down to her toes, just as she had known it would.

Jared lay down on top of his sleeping bag and clasped his hands behind his head. He tried to remember any previous cases of participants being abducted from an expedition. He vaguely remembered rumors of an ex-husband coming after his wife. They had ended up reconciling and she had left with him. He doubted that would be the case if anyone came after Kendra. If anyone did, it would be because they were more than a little ticked off. He glanced over at his partner, Phil, and decided against waking him at this hour. *Time enough to fill him in tomorrow.* Jared sighed again. This trip was beginning to feel more and more like a *lose.*

SueAnn's stirring early the next morning brought Kendra to a sitting position. She rubbed her eyes and looked over at the perky redhead.

"How's the ankle?"

SueAnn looked up. Her eyes were wide and hopeful. "Well, right now it feels great. Soaking it in witch hazel worked wonders."

"We'll wrap it tightly before you put on your boots and you should be all right. If you had been wearing those boots yesterday, you probably wouldn't have twisted it."

SueAnn wrinkled her pert nose. "Yeah, I've heard that before. Somehow, I didn't think the first day would be quite so tough."

"What did you think it would be? *A social, get to know each other, kind of day?*" Kendra pushed herself off her sleeping bag.

"Something like that." SueAnn looked at Kendra, whispered conspiratorially, "Don't you think Phil is a hunk?"

Kendra stared at her, trying vainly to remember what Phil looked like. As for herself, she had had eyes only for Jared Hall.

"Yeah, right. Is that why you're here, SueAnn?"

"Not exactly. I do want something that challenges me. But after one look at Phil, I realized that getting him to notice me might be the biggest challenge of my life."

Kendra narrowed her eyes. "When you slipped yesterday, you were just in front of him. Were you, by chance, trying to get his attention then?"

SueAnn gasped. "Of course not. You were there. You saw what happened. The rock face crumbled."

"Just checking, because, SueAnn, I don't think that's the way to get his attention. Impress him with cunning and intelligence, not with weakness."

"Is that your strategy?" SueAnn asked.

Kendra glanced at her. "I beg your pardon?"

"With Jared? I noticed he couldn't keep his eyes off you yesterday."

Kendra swallowed. "I'm afraid I didn't notice."

"But you snuck out to meet him last night. I saw you coming back together."

"I couldn't sleep. Neither could he. He came up on me and we talked for a while, then we walked back."

"Yeah, right." SueAnn threw her words back at her.

Kendra laughed. "All right, my friend, Jared is definitely a hunk. Unfortunately, I don't have time or space for anyone in my life at the moment."

"We'll see," SueAnn said with a knowing smile. "Now, how about wrapping my ankle? I have to convince our hunks that I can keep up."

"Can you, SueAnn?" Kendra asked. "Because I won't be party to causing you further injury."

"I'm fine. Really."

Kendra searched her face, saw openness and a slight hurt that Kendra would question her.

"All right," she sighed. "Just don't make me regret this."

"Now that's a lovely sight," Phil Thomas said as he stood beside Jared.

Jared turned to see Kendra and SueAnn emerge from their tent. So far no one else had stirred. In five minutes, they would blow a whistle. In thirty minutes, they would be on the trail.

Jared frowned. "What exactly do you find so lovely?"

"SueAnn walking normally. I was afraid she would have to leave the expedition." Phil glanced at Jared. "What did you think I meant?" His gaze followed Jared's. "Un-huh. Too tall. Too athletic. Too—"

"—*perfect*," Jared supplied.

"That, too," Phil admitted. "But you know me. A lady like Kendra scares me to death."

"I have it on good authority that that makes you part of a sizable majority," Jared drawled.

"How big a majority?" Phil asked.

"About ninety-nine to one."

"And you're the one?"

Jared glanced at his partner. "'Fraid not. I've gotten soft since I left the military."

"Yeah, right."

CHAPTER TWO

Kendra leaned against a tree, chest heaving, and pulled out her canteen.

"I thought at least you would have enough sense to pace yourself!"

Kendra recognized the cold voice and turned to look at the speaker. "Sorry to disappoint you, Major. I—"

"Stop calling me Major. No one else knows my military status. Ex-military status," Jared corrected.

Kendra held his gaze for a moment, shrugged. "Sorry. Jared just seems a little too cozy. I mean, first names are usually for friends."

"Have it your way," he said. "Now, would you care to explain why you broke a speed record climbing up out of that ravine?"

Kendra shivered. "I'm claustrophobic—and I had to get back into the sunlight. I'm sorry. I know it's stupid—"

To her surprise, he put a hand on her arm. "Take it easy. Why didn't you tell me?"

"Tell you what?" His hand was warm against her bare arm and Kendra tried to ignore the chaos it caused with her nerve endings.

"A lot of participants come here to try and overcome certain fears. Claustrophobia is a common one. We can take it more slowly, not hit you with it all at once."

"I always figured if anyone knew, they would have an advantage—use it against me." Kendra wet her lips.

"I would say you have a problem with trust, too," Jared said quietly. "*Everyone*, or just me?"

Kendra pulled her arm free and sipped from her canteen. "Not everyone, but not just you, either."

"But you don't trust me. I wonder why. Was it something that happened in Kuwait?"

"Could we just drop this subject?" Kendra asked as her fellow expedition members began to crawl up from the ravine.

"For the moment. *But not forever*, Ms. Allen."

Jared turned his attention to the other women now collapsed around them. At that moment, Phil and SueAnn brought up the rear.

"Okay, everyone, take five. Then we have a slow hike for a couple of miles to cool off before lunch." Jared threw a meaningful glance at Kendra. "This part of the trail is easy. Conserve your energy. It gets a lot tougher after lunch."

With that he sat down on a boulder under a tree and was quickly surrounded by a half dozen sweaty, panting women. Kendra found herself alone under her tree when she wanted nothing more than to seek out Jared's company herself. She glanced around to see Phil with SueAnn and a couple of other women sprawled on the grass under another tree. She raised her canteen to her lips and tried to swallow the tepid water around the lump in her throat.

"What do you expect?" she asked herself in disgust. "You just told him you don't trust him. Why would he want to be around you?"

Jared glanced over at Kendra slumped against the tree, saw her swipe a hand across her eyes. He frowned. He hadn't meant to be so tough on her, but her revelation that she didn't trust him struck a nerve. What reason could she have for not trusting him?

He tried to follow the conversation going on around him, but all the while his concentration was focused a few feet away on one very complicated and frightened woman.

A woman who was getting under his skin seemingly without even trying.

And that would have to be a lose. The last win he'd had where a woman was concerned had been over ten years ago.

"That's better," Jared said as he caught up to Kendra after a short lunch break. "I'm sorry I was so hard on you earlier. As I've explained before, it's my job to see that no one gets hurt."

Kendra glanced at him, but said nothing. Turning back to the trail, she continued walking.

"Come on, Kendra, talk to me," Jared coaxed. "You obviously have some expectations of this program. You—"

"You know my expectations, and it isn't going to happen!"

"You're here to hide out, nothing more?"

"That's very good, Maj--Jared. To hide out and participate enough to blend in."

"And miss so many opportunities," he said. "Won't you reconsider your degree of participation? You might find something you enjoy."

At that moment SueAnn's laughter rang out and Kendra stumbled over a root. Jared's hand shot out to catch her.

"Careful!" he murmured. "It would seem that SueAnn has found something she enjoys." *As much as he enjoyed touching Kendra, he wondered.*

"Phil's attention," Kendra said. "I'm beginning to wonder if she hurt her ankle at all." She shook off his hand and moved out of reach.

"So it isn't just men you don't trust," Jared observed. "I was beginning to wonder."

She shot him a venomous look and Jared grinned. "Come on, lady. This could be a long two weeks if you insist on hanging on to this attitude."

"Or you could simply find someone else to hit on," Kendra suggested.

He chuckled, not bothering to deny it. "Un-huh. No one else is worth my time."

Kendra increased her speed and Jared touched her arm again. "Slow down," he growled. "You might be able to hold this pace but the others can't, especially SueAnn."

Kendra gave an exaggerated sigh and slowed to what seemed a crawl. "Look, I have things on my mind, all right? Couldn't you go talk to Phil or something?"

"Not if you insist on taking the lead like this. One of us has to be out front, one brings up the rear."

"I can't go back there and listen to that incessant chatter. If I hear Louella explain one more time why her hair looks so great—"

Jared smothered a grin. "Her hair does look great—and she owns a chain of beauty supply stores. Why shouldn't she talk about it? The others seem interested."

"Then why don't you go back and listen to her. I promise not to get in trouble up here by myself. I won't even get out of sight."

"No deal. I'd rather listen to you."

"I haven't been talking."

"So I've noticed. So has everyone else. You have to try, Kendra. I know you're a good actress. You're job proves it."

She stopped suddenly, turning to him. "Just let me walk out alone, okay? I know enough to survive. I can't get involved with these women. I could be putting them in danger. I will—"

"No. I told you we'll be meeting up with the others in a few hours."

"So what does that mean? *That I'll be putting even more people in danger.*"

"Kendra, come off it," he warned. "No on is in danger. If I thought there was a chance of that, I'd abort the whole expedition now."

So why couldn't he shake the sense of impending doom he'd felt since last night?

"Fine." Her troubled gray eyes held his. Her voice had fallen even lower, making the huskiness more pronounced. She swallowed and blinked away a sheen of tears. "You don't believe me. I wonder what ever made me think you were different!"

Jared stared at her, feeling the words pierce his soul. He tried once more to reason with her. "Look, Kendra, I know about danger. You're going to be all right."

"Yeah, right!" She turned away and began walking again as the rest of the group approached.

Jared let several of the women pass him before falling in step, being careful to keep Kendra in sight. Maybe it would be better, after all, to give her some space.

And him time to figure out what was going on.

Kendra tried to still her trembling, the pounding of her heart. Was she overreacting? She had the most uncanny feeling that she was being watched, and not by Jared. She knew that as far as he was concerned, she was making a fool of herself. He didn't believe her, thought her hysterical. Okay, so she was on her own. She knew how to survive. It would just be so much easier if she didn't have to worry about anyone else.

Jared glanced up to see that Kendra had let the group overtake her. She slowed her pace until she fell behind the others. He adjusted his step and found himself beside her.

"I need to talk to you," Kendra said under her breath.

"So talk."

"I'm leaving the group. I'm walking out by myself."

"Kendra—" he broke off in exasperation and she went on before he could collect his thoughts.

"I didn't have to tell you. I could have just turned off the trail. But then you might have felt compelled to look for me."

"Thanks for your consideration."

Kendra flinched. "You've expressed your contempt well, Major. But you've been out of the military for several years. Maybe you've lost your edge. All I know is that I've had to depend on my instincts to survive for the last twelve years, and right now they're telling me that I'm headed full speed toward disaster."

"Really. The program isn't that hard," he drawled.

She sighed. "You know I'm not talking about the program."

"Go on."

"I didn't tell you about my last job. I went to Germany to check out a nuclear weapons plant. I'm fairly up on international terrorism, and the two guys who were on my case fit every profile I've studied. The night before I left, when I decided I had to cut my losses, I overheard them discussing me, that I knew too much, and what they thought they should do about it."

Jared felt his pulse quicken, but tried not to show it. "So you expect a couple of current or former *Baader-Meinhof* members to show up here in the middle of the Colorado Rockies and kidnap you. To what end?"

"Not for ransom, I'm sure of that. Just to eliminate me on the off chance I might indeed know too much."

"Does the word paranoid mean anything to you, Kendra? Have you considered it might be time for another line of work?"

To his surprise she smiled. "Several times during the last two days." She sobered. "I'm sorry. Don't take this personally, but I have to go."

"I can't let you."

"You can't stop me."

At that moment, Jared's radio crackled and he reached for it, stopping short on the trail.

"Hall here. Over."

"Double E. Hall, we have a situation. Over."

Jared rolled his eyes. "What kind of situation? Over."

"Smith and Payne with their tour are supposed to meet your group tonight. Correct?"

"Roger that."

"They've had a couple of defections."

"*Defections?*" Jared felt the skin crawl on the back of his neck. Beside him, he felt Kendra tense and reached out to clasp her arm.

"When we got the report and checked them out, it turns out they were also imposters."

Jared felt his fingers tighten around Kendra's wrist. He wet his lips, not sure how to proceed.

"So what am I supposed to do?" he asked, his mind going over his own possibilities.

"I'm not sure. I just felt you should have the information. Their names are Karl Weiner and Eric Bruener and they split just before lunch. The main group is still about seven miles to your south. They may be harmless and just got tired of the program. Over."

"Here's what I need you to do," Jared said, still holding Kendra who had not yet struggled, but was staring at him, eyes huge in her pale face. "Round up the first four instructors you can find and drop them at the camp site before we get there. Have them stay out of sight and then blend in so that neither group knows they aren't with the other. Any questions? Over."

"What's up, Hall?"

"We have a *situation* here. Perhaps related. I'll fill you in later. Hall, over and out."

Jared put the radio back on his belt and turned to Kendra. He could feel her trembling. His hand slid down her wrist to her hand, then he caught the other and brought them together inside his.

"I'm sorry I didn't believe you," he whispered. *"Or myself.* You were right last night when you asked if I was expecting trouble. I had a feeling— nothing specific."

Kendra tried to speak, wet her lips. "It is rather fantastic, isn't it?" From the huskiness in her voice, it was just on the edge of breaking.

Without thinking of the consequences, Jared pulled her into his arms.

"I have to go," Kendra whispered.

"I can't let you." His hands stroked her back, calming, soothing.

"I can't put anyone else in danger, including you."

"I can't let you go, Kendra." He held her away to look into her eyes. "Not when I've just realized you're everything I never even knew I wanted."

She lifted a hand to touch his face, stroked his jaw, rough from two days without shaving.

"Wrong time. Wrong place. Isn't that what life's about?" she said.

"It doesn't have to be."

She shook her head. "I'm afraid it does this time."

"Kendra." He speared his fingers into her hair and pulled her face to his. "I've been wanting to do this," he murmured as his lips closed over hers.

Kendra's tentative struggles quickly turned into response as her lips moved to answer his. Her arms slipped around his neck.

Jared groaned and fought the desire that surged through him like wildfire. He raised his head and held her a little away.

"*Wrong place*, in any case," he rasped.

Her eyes searched his, the beginnings of desire washed away by fear.

"Jared, someone is watching us."

He jerked erect, then casually pulled her back into his arms, her head nestled against his shoulder.

"Anything else?"

"Just that I first felt it about an hour ago. I didn't tell you because—you were already upset enough with me."

"Any feel from which direction? *Anything* that might help?"

With her cheek pressed to his neck, she let her eyes search the area. Finally, across a ravine among some rocks, she saw a flash of light.

"Possible binoculars to the southeast. I just saw the sun reflect off something. There. I saw it again."

Jared slowly turned with her still locked in his embrace. "Remind me to recruit you for my next mission."

"I wouldn't miss it."

"Two sets, actually. About six feet apart." He stepped back, then turned her, sliding an arm across her shoulder. "We join the others for a quick break while I bring Phil up to speed."

Kendra stopped in her tracks. "I can't let you."

Jared turned back. "I lead this mission, love, and everyone obeys, and no one is sacrificed." He started her forward again. "What do you know about Double E?"

"Double E?" She looked puzzled. "Oh, you mean *Extreme Expeditions*? Obviously, not much."

"It's my company. I started it five years ago with a dozen of my buddies in the service. Since then, another dozen have joined us. All my instructors are late from Special Forces. There will be four of us here already, and four more are joining us. I think we will be able to handle a couple of *Baader-Meinhof* wannabes."

Kendra trembled. "At what cost? Don't you see—"

"They know where you are. I can't let you go. If you leave they will go straight after you, and from your description of their intentions, ruling out ransom, well, that's not in the cards. You aren't leaving."

"Shouldn't you at least discuss this with your buddies—at least Phil—get a second opinion?"

"I don't have to. I know what they will say. As crude as it sounds, love, we need you as bait. If these guys are desperate enough to follow you from Germany and track you here, they have to be wanted for something. I'm afraid all of us have a highly over-developed sense of civic responsibility."

Kendra stared at him for long seconds, then her lips twitched. "*Geez*. And I thought for a moment there that you cared." She turned away.

Jared put a hand on her shoulder and spun her around into his arms. He pulled her close. *"Hold that thought."* His mouth found hers again, almost desperately this time.

When he released her, Kendra looked drugged, and thoroughly kissed. He watched as she slowly opened her eyes and focused on him.

"Oh, Jared," she whispered.

He brushed his thumb across her lips. "Yes, love," he said around the huskiness in his own voice. He took her arm to hurry down the trail.

CHAPTER THREE

Kendra felt she would snap from the tension at any moment. As soon as she and Jared rejoined the group, he sought out Phil and they remained deep in discussion for several minutes. Jared pulled out his radio and held a consultation with Double E headquarters, apparently making slight modifications to his earlier plan. Then he pocketed his radio, winked at Kendra and continued as if nothing was amiss. The campsite was only a couple of miles away, but she thought she might explode long before they reached it.

Someone touched her arm and she jerked around. "SueAnn! Sorry. You startled me. How's the ankle?"

"A fine time to ask, but it's all right."

"Good. And how's Phil?"

"Better than all right," SueAnn said with a wicked grin. "How's Jared?"

Kendra tensed. "How would I know?"

"First hand experience from what I saw. Phil sent me back to check on you two, but when I saw that you were in good hands, literally speaking, I snuck back without disturbing you."

Kendra again decided that nonchalance was her best cover. She gave an elegant shrug. "Is that jealously I hear, my friend, or wistfulness?"

"Both," SueAnn crinkled her nose adorably. "Tell me your secret. How did you work so fast?"

Searching for an answer, Kendra realized that the truth itself was so fantastic, no one would believe it.

"Well," she began, "this lady spy is being chased by international terrorists, and a handsome major from Special Forces comes to her rescue—"

SueAnn giggled. "What do you do, anyway, Kendra? You haven't told us. Are you a writer? *Suspense thrillers? Romance?*"

Kendra laughed and decided to play along. "Unpublished so far, so I can't quit my day job just yet."

"I knew it!" SueAnn squealed. "There's something about you, like you are on another plane of existence. I guess that's when you get your ideas for stories, huh?"

"Something like that," Kendra said, realizing this, too, was almost the truth. "My mother always called me a dreamer. I guess that's what she meant."

"Wow! I envy you." SueAnn stared at her in something akin to awe.

Kendra's mouth fell open. *"You envy me?"*

"Yes," she sighed. "I don't have a creative bone in my body. My whole world is so technical I don't believe I've used the right side of my brain since I was forced to do finger painting in kindergarten."

"Oh, come on!" Kendra laughed. "What could be that technical?"

In a heartbeat, SueAnn's whole demeanor changed. "I'm not really supposed to tell anyone. It's highly secret. But somehow I feel that I can trust you. I make nuclear weapons. My boss thought I was on the verge of burnout and paid for me to come here to work off some stress."

Kendra felt her heartbeat slow down, believed she could feel the blood as it coursed through her veins. She seemed to be moving in slow motion. Who was the mysterious "S" in her notes? SueAnn? She wet her lips.

"I know it is against the rules, we're supposed to only be on a first name basis, but would you trust me a little further and tell me your last name, SueAnn?"

SueAnn frowned. "Is something wrong, Kendra? You have a funny look on your face."

"Answer her, SueAnn," Jared spoke behind her. "It's all right. Tell her your last name. Your code name, too, if you have one."

SueAnn looked from Jared to Kendra. "My last name is Talmidge. My code name," she paused, ran a hand through her russet curls, "is Spitfire."

Kendra looked at Jared and knew he could see the horror on her face.

"Leave us, SueAnn," he said. "Kendra and I have to talk."

"No." Kendra held up her hand. "She needs to hear this. I may be wrong about who they're really after."

"Kendra!" Jared exploded. "I wish we could have discussed this first."

SueAnn looked at Kendra. "That bit about a lady spy? That wasn't just a story to brush me off, was it?"

Kendra sighed, decided to ignore Jared. "SueAnn, does the acronym 'DKW' mean anything to you, as in *Deutschen Kern Werks*?"

"Of course. The German Nuclear Works. We had a couple of guys in on an exchange program right after the Wall fell. I've even gotten a couple of emails from them over the years."

"Don't tell me that's where you've been?" Jared spoke to Kendra.

"Spitfire was the one piece I was still missing. They didn't have everything they needed, either, but if they get her, they will have."

"And where do you fit in?" Jared asked.

"I don't know. Maybe I don't. Maybe you should prepare to be flexible." She turned to face him. "And one thing you need to keep in mind. *I'm expendable.*"

"Not likely—" Jared began, his eyes snapping in anger.

"Yes, likely. We both serve our country. You know as well as I do what the priorities are here."

"We'll talk about this later. We should move on. Everything is ready at the camp."

Kendra held his gaze. *"Everything?"*

"Everything. Trust me, love."

A festive mood pervaded the camp as tents were pitched and dinner preparations began. Jared's reinforcements timed their arrival perfectly, so as not to arouse suspicion from anyone except the instructors from the second expedition, who were quickly enlightened by Jared.

Kendra kept an eye on proceedings as she threw herself into the dinner detail in order to have some place to channel her energies. She had been cautioned to act naturally, and not to spend too much time with SueAnn, who seemed to be holding up admirably under the circumstances. Along the same line, Jared and Phil were doing their best not to pay extra attention to either Kendra or SueAnn.

Looking around, Kendra noticed first one and then all four of the new instructors gradually drift away from camp. Jared had told her he would be posting a guard. She glanced over at their tent and its proximity to that of Jared and Phil on one side and of Smith and Payne on the other. All were slightly apart from the remaining tents.

Kendra knew that none of them would sleep tonight, including those on guard. She had never been good at waiting and felt the muscles tightening in her neck and the beginnings of a migraine.

"Relax, love." The whisper of sound came from her right and Kendra turned. She wanted to step into Jared's arms and lose herself in the comfort they offered, but didn't dare. Instead she let her eyes tell him everything she felt, everything she desired.

Jared chuckled. "Don't look at me like that once this is over, my sweet," he warned. "You may not be ready for the consequences."

Kendra wet her lips. "Get me out of this and you can name your price."

Jared's gaze cooled and when he spoke, the ice in his voice startled her. "Not quite what I had in mind. I don't usually seek favors in return for doing my job." He turned on his heel and strode away.

Kendra stared after him. *Now what did I say?* she murmured aloud.

"He's a lot more than just a handsome major from Special Forces, isn't he?" SueAnn asked beside her.

Kendra turned, nodded. "How do these things happen, SueAnn? One day you feel you're in control of your life. The next you meet someone like Jared Hall, and all the walls come tumbling down."

34

SueAnn giggled, sounding more like her old self. "Why don't you ask me about something easy, like nuclear fusion or the origin of the universe?"

Kendra laughed, feeling some of the tension ease. "You know something, SueAnn Talmidge, you are quite a woman. I wish I had met you before this."

"So, we keep in touch from now on. You can be my maid of honor. Or matron, as the case may be."

Kendra straightened to throw her a glance.

"Well," SueAnn grinned. "You might land Jared before I snare Phil."

"Yeah," Kendra said. "Except I don't believe it is open season on mercenaries. And do we really want one?"

"That's a cruel thing to say!" SueAnn gasped, her eyes wide.

"But valid, none the less."

"You're just afraid of what you're feeling," SueAnn said. "I see the way you look at him, Kendra."

"Do we have to talk about this?"

SueAnn perched on a camp stool. "It's better than the only other subject that comes to mind, don't you think?"

Kendra laughed. "I'll give you that." She sighed. "Yes, I'm afraid, and any other time, any other place, Jared Hall wouldn't know what hit him."

"Then hold tight to those feelings. This will be over, Kendra."

Kendra stirred the cornbread batter one final time before pouring it into skillets and putting them over hot coals as she had been instructed.

"So," she asked, "how are things going with Phil? I noticed you bringing up the rear most of the day."

"That way I had him to myself," SueAnn smirked. "I don't think he knows what hit him."

"I always admire a person who knows what they want and how to get it," Kendra drawled.

"Is that maybe because you don't know?"

Kendra sat back on her heels to study SueAnn. "If I had to guess, I'd say you probably have a degree in physics, chemistry, engineering and psychology, with at least a couple of them advanced."

SueAnn grinned. *"Three out of four.* I only minored in chemistry. I have a master's in physics and a doctorate in psychology. Psychological profiles are very important in my field."

"I would hope so," Kendra said, still looking at SueAnn in awe. "But the helpless redhead routine still throws me. Why? It must be so out of character."

"That's how I relax. It saves my sanity. When I go to work, I get so involved that I forget to eat, forget to sleep, forget to call my mother." She winced. "When I manage to get away, I do a mind dump. I forget everything, even how to put gas in my car."

"That must be a useful talent. I could do with a mind dump about now," Kendra said wistfully.

"Not just yet," SueAnn said. "I think you're burning my dinner."

Kendra scrambled to save the meal and flipped the batter in the pans to discover only minor scorching on the bottom. *Would she never get the hang of this cooking thing?*

"You owe me," SueAnn grinned as she got to her feet. "I also have a superior sense of smell."

Kendra wrinkled her nose before an answering smile touched her lips.

Jared stood again and watched the sunset, wondering what the night would bring. He waited until darkness had fallen completely, then turned slowly to see flickers from four tiny pen lights, about as conspicuous as fireflies. All was in order around the camp. The guards were alert and in place.

Kendra sank back on her bedroll, feeling the tension building again. She wanted to run screaming from the tent, through the camp and into the woods. A whisper of sound at the opening of the tent brought her upright, a hand going to her mouth.

Phil stuck his head in, followed by a hand as he reached for SueAnn. He looked at Kendra.

"I didn't mean to frighten you," he whispered. "I came to switch roommates with you."

Kendra watched in stunned amazement as Phil led SueAnn from the tent. A moment later Jared slipped in and let the flap close.

Kendra drew her knees up and rested her chin on them as she watched Jared settle on SueAnn's sleeping bag. Her eyes adjusted until she could make out his features. He was watching her.

"Are you going to come over here?" Jared growled. "Or do I move over there?"

Kendra cleared her throat. "I don't know. What exactly do you have in mind?" She rubbed her neck, a different kind of tension building now.

"Oh, you look like you could use a massage about now. You're wound so tight, I'm afraid you're gonna break."

She let her hand drop. "If you touch me, I very well may break."

"I promise to be gentle. I give great neck rubs, or so I've been told."

"Thanks, but I'll pass." A neck massage sounded wonderful, but Kendra wanted his touch so badly, she knew that would never be enough.

"You don't know what you're missing," he warned. Kendra could hear the teasing in his voice.

"Probably not." She lay back, clasping her hands behind her head. After a moment she turned on her side, her back to him.

"Kendra, I—"

"Shouldn't we be quiet?" she asked. "I mean, if anyone hears you, they might not come, right?"

"Love, if anyone gets near camp, my men have failed to do their jobs."

"But—you said I was bait?" Her voice trembled. "How can you take them in if they don't actually attempt something?"

"*Justifiable suspicion.* I had them run through the computer and got a call back about an hour ago. They have some very unpleasant associates. My men are to secure them on sight. A military chopper will be here at first light."

"And if they don't come tonight?"

He moved across to her sleeping bag and stretched out beside her. She opened her eyes as he slipped his arms around her.

"Relax," he whispered. "Let me do all the worrying."

"That's easy for you to say," she murmured, succumbing to the comfort and security of having him next to her.

He dropped a kiss on the back of her neck. "And easy for you to do. Go to sleep, love. In the morning it will all be over."

"Jared?"

"What now?" She felt his sigh.

"How did you find out they were imposters?"

He stiffened slightly against her, relaxed again. "The real Karl and Eric were found bound and gagged in their apartment by Karl's sister. She called Double E, knowing they were supposed to be on expedition." His voice sounded wooden, forced.

"Thank God that was all. I'm so glad they're still alive." Kendra swallowed hard.

Jared was silent for a second too long. Kendra stirred, then sat up. "They are still alive, aren't they? Or did I just assume—"

"I'm sorry, Kendra. They were—executed. A bullet in the back of the head. I didn't want to tell you. You have enough to deal with as it is."

She lay back as a slow trembling began to consume her. She thrust her hands into her hair and curled into a fetal position.

"Dear God, no! Please, God, no!"

"Kendra." The gentleness in Jared's voice proved to be her undoing. She felt tears slide down her cheeks, followed by huge gulping sobs.

Jared pulled her into his arms and she clung to him in mindless need, until finally the tears stopped, followed by a numbing exhaustion.

With a final trembling sigh, Kendra fell asleep in his arms, and Jared reached up to brush at the moisture on his own lashes. It tore him apart to see her so shattered. Death was no stranger to him, he had seen too much of it in his time. He had both faced it and dealt it as time and place dictated. He had constructed a place in his mind to file away such matters for more careful examination at a later date. Kendra had no such buffer. She would also be blaming herself, however misdirected that blame, for the deaths of the expedition members.

Besides his men, twenty other military and law enforcement officers waited nearby to assist in the arrest. It no longer mattered whether Kendra and SueAnn were potential targets or not. *These men were wanted for capital murder.*

He carefully placed Kendra back against her pillow and stretched out beside her, an arm crooked beneath his head. She was as safe as he could make her. He reached over to drag his back pack closer and pulled out a Colt .45. He checked the safety and placed it within easy reach. No one got to her without going through him first.

CHAPTER FOUR

A loud drumming vibration shook Kendra awake and she sat with heart pounding until she realized she heard the turning rotors of a helicopter. She looked around. *Jared was gone!* Simultaneously, she realized that dawn had broken. She crawled to the opening of the tent and pushed the flap aside.

Jared stood with his back to her, deep in conversation with a man in full military dress and M16 rifle. Kendra could not suppress a shudder and her gaze shifted to the two men sitting on the other side of the campfire.

It took a moment for her to process what seemed unusual about them. Then she realized they were sitting back to back, tied together with a single rope. Their feet were bound, and their hands shackled together on each side with handcuffs. She could see the side of one face and it appeared to be bruised and bloody. She frowned as she tried to make out identifying features. *Were these the same men she had worked with, who thought she knew too much?*

Kendra had experienced a moment of elation that they had been caught, but now she shuddered in revulsion. She saw a movement out of the corner of her eye and then Phil striding toward her. Though casually dressed, he could not conceal the toughness he exuded. His camp shirt and shorts may as well have been military fatigues. He knelt in front of her tent, shielding her from view.

"Are you all right, Kendra?" His voice was surprisingly gentle.

She didn't answer that question, but asked one of her own. "You caught them, right? You're sure they're the ones?"

"We aren't leaving anything to chance. Of course, they aren't talking, but our intelligence indicates they were working alone."

Kendra shuddered again. Phil put a hand on her shoulder.

"Please stay out of sight, Kendra. I've already talked to SueAnn. There's no reason to give them the satisfaction of knowing they were on target. You might want to pack up. We'll be leaving as soon as the Huey lifts off."

Kendra stared at him. "You mean we just go on as if nothing happened. How do you explain this to the others?" She glanced around at the huddled groups in the early morning chill.

"They will be told the truth. Or as close to it as we dare. Jared and I, with you and SueAnn, will leave on one of our choppers as soon as the military clears out. We have to go back and answer a few questions. Our replacements will be onboard our chopper."

"So it's all over." Kendra spoke to herself.

"It looks that way. It all went exactly as Jared planned." He gave a slight grin. "Sometimes I don't know what to make of him. We've been together a long time. He's uncanny in how well he knows the criminal mind."

42

Kendra did not reply. She had been thinking along much those same lines herself.

Phil dropped the flap and turned away. Kendra quickly got her things together and rolled up her sleeping bag. As she moved about the darkened interior of the tent, she tripped over something and bent to pick up Jared's back pack. The flap fell open and she caught a metallic glint. She peered closer and suddenly the backpack thudded to the floor at her feet.

"Yes, Kendra, I always carry a gun." Jared's voice came from the doorway, cold and unyielding. "I've seen too much for too long to ever be caught without one."

She whirled to stare at him, could think of nothing to say, and the seconds grew into an eternity. She wet her lips. "Is it over?"

"It's over. Are you ready to leave?"

She nodded, and ducked past him out the door. He disappeared inside and came back out with his backpack and SueAnn's bedroll.

"What about the tent?"

"Phil will take care of that. I'll get you aboard."

"Where are you taking me?"

"Home, if that's practical, for a change of clothes. If not, we go shopping. You and SueAnn are meeting with representatives from her company and the Pentagon at ten o'clock tomorrow."

"A debriefing."

"I see you know the routine."

"Will I be able to call someone? My boss?"

"Of course." He put his hand on the back of her head as they ducked under the turning rotors and she climbed up into the waiting helicopter. There

43

was no sign of the Huey or that it had ever existed.

Kendra paused to look down at SueAnn in a seat by a window.

"Are you all right?" Kendra asked.

SueAnn made an attempt at a smile. "Sure."

"Would you mind if I sit here?" The moment she asked, Kendra regretted the question.

SueAnn looked striken. "I—" she stammered.

"Right. *Phil.*" Kendra was already moving away. "I'll just find a place back here."

Jared paused for a moment to speak with SueAnn and Kendra found a seat by a window and dropped her backpack on the seat next to her. Then Jared was beside her, stowing his backpack and reaching down for hers.

"Funny thing about human nature," he mused. "How the same situation can bring some people closer and drive others apart." He looked down at her for a moment, piercing dark eyes veiled by thick black lashes. Then he gave a careless shrug and dropped down on the bench seat behind her. "This looks like a good place to try and get some sleep."

Kendra closed her eyes but could not shut out his image. In battered boots, black jeans and an olive T-shirt, he looked tough, male and irresistible. The conflict in her soul threatened to tear her apart.

Sighing, Kendra gave in to the urge to look back at Jared. He sprawled across the seat, hands clasped behind his head. His eyes were closed, lashes fanning across his high cheek bones. A lock of dark hair fell across his forehead. His aristocratic nose had a slight kink near the bridge as if perhaps it had been broken. Then her gaze dropped to his mouth and Kendra swallowed. Firm and chiseled, she knew how those lips felt on hers, how they tasted.

Jared opened his eyes. "See anything you like?"

Kendra felt her cheeks grow warm, but held his gaze. She nodded slowly. "I do. I just don't know what I would do with it."

He closed his eyes. "Then, perhaps, little girl, you shouldn't go shopping until you know the value of the merchandise."

Kendra turned to stare out the window, mortified. Was she being naive? Before she could sink into further introspection, Phil bounded aboard, grabbed a thermos of coffee from behind the pilot and told him to lift off.

Phil proceeded to hand out coffee and donuts to everyone, including the pilot, whom he addressed as Mark. Jared leaned forward in his seat and Phil sat sideways so they could talk.

Kendra felt a momentary stab of pity for SueAnn and pretended not to listen to the conversation. It only lasted a couple of minutes, however, and Phil turned back to SueAnn, leaning over to whisper in her ear. The stab of pity turned into loneliness such as she had never felt before when Phil put his arm across SueAnn's shoulders and she snuggled against him.

Unwilling to look back at Jared, and wanting to give Phil and SueAnn privacy, Kendra kept her gaze fixed on the scenery below. Although beautiful, it could not hold her attention, and she found herself remembering strong, comforting arms, and breath warm against her neck.

Jared watched Kendra through veiled lashes as he pretended to sleep. He again felt the stab of hurt as he watched her withdraw from him at sight of the gun, saw her judging and condemning him. *How did she think they had managed to turn things around last night and get the drop on the would-be abductors?*

He leaned forward, touched her shoulder, felt her jump, then shrink away from him.

"Where's home?"

She looked at him. "Seattle." The husky voice that drove him wild was even more so now with strain.

He shook his head. "I'm afraid we don't have time for that. We can go somewhere tonight and you can buy clothes for tomorrow."

"Where are we now?"

"Approaching Denver."

Her eyes lighted with interest. "I checked a bag with clothes for my return trip in Denver. I didn't know if I would be returning home right away, so I came prepared."

"Good, you can pick it up while I book our flights to D.C." He moved to the seat beside Kendra and leaned forward to tap Phil on the shoulder. "What's SueAnn's situation for tomorrow?"

Phil turned his head. "She's going to call her Mom from Denver and have her send a bag with her boss."

Jared nodded. "Then I guess we have everything covered."

Phil threw a glance at Kendra, then back at Jared. "How's everything back there?"

"A little chilly," Jared said as he returned to his seat. "I'll ask Mark to have the air conditioning checked."

He saw Kendra flinch, then turn back to look out the window.

On the ground in Denver, after what to Kendra had been an interminable flight, she watched as Jared and Phil quickly collected the backpacks. They left the tents and bedrolls on board the helicopter and told Mark to meet them again in a couple of days.

46

"I'll book the flights," Jared said, walking backward in front of the others. "Kendra, find your bag, and SueAnn make your call. We should just be able to make the 11:00 flight to D.C., so we may have to hustle. I'll page you, Phil, with the gate number."

Phil gave a salute and Jared moved off, walking quickly with long, sure strides. Kendra was so engrossed in watching him that she stumbled and Phil caught her arm.

"Careful," he warned. "The scenery around here is great, but there are many pitfalls for the unsuspecting."

Kendra threw him a glance, looking for some hidden meaning behind his words. The glance he returned was all blue-eyed innocence, yet still managed to warn her to watch her step, figuratively speaking.

Kendra dug the key out of her bag and fumbled with the lock on the storage vault. SueAnn leaned casually against the wall beside her.

"What's with you this morning?" SueAnn demanded without warning. "You're treating Jared as if he has the plague."

"I'd rather not talk about it."

"You need to talk about it," SueAnn insisted.

"Look, don't you charge for your advice, Doctor? I can't afford you." Kendra jerked her bag out of the locker and turned away.

SueAnn fell into step beside her. "Oh, sometimes I take on a charity case if it interests me. This one does."

"Shouldn't you be calling your mother?" Kendra reminded.

"I can do that from the plane," she replied. "Now, back to you and Jared. Give."

"I saw a gun in his backpack this morning," Kendra said, unable to meet SueAnn's eyes.

"Is that all?" SueAnn asked, obviously puzzled.

"It's enough." Kendra moved on.

"Well, since you referred to him as a mercenary, maybe it is. *For you.* Are you perhaps confusing guns with the evil people who sometimes use them and condemning Jared by association? Might I remind you that without Jared, who knows what would have happened to you and me last night?"

Kendra didn't want to think about that. She waved her hand in dismissal. "Oh, Phil would have saved you!"

"No. He couldn't have. Not by himself."

Kendra stopped short, staring at SueAnn. *"Say that again."*

"Phil makes a great follower," SueAnn explained, "especially when he has a leader like Jared. But he doesn't take charge and make things happen. *That's Jared."*

Kendra still stared at her. "And you want a man like that?"

SueAnn grinned wickedly. "Sure. Why not? I know how to take charge and make things happen."

Kendra laughed, breaking the tension. Impulsively, she reached over to hug SueAnn. "Where have you been all my life? I could have used a friend with your perspective."

"Yeah?" SueAnn returned the hug. "Well, now you have one." She held Kendra at arm's length. "So how about telling me the real problem here?"

"Are you sure you want to know? I'm sure as a psychologist you'll have a field day with this." Kendra watched SueAnn, giving her a chance to change her mind.

"Give." SueAnn smiled her encouragement.

Kendra looked down, feeling the old knots of tension in her stomach. She drew a deep breath. "When I was sixteen, my nine year old brother blew his head off with a neighbor's gun. I was supposed to be babysitting for my neighbor's son and my brother. I—" Kendra felt her self swaying and her voice sounded a long way off.

SueAnn grabbed her arm and pulled her over to a row of seats. She sat down beside her and forced her head down.

"Take a deep breath," SueAnn said. "Feeling better?"

Kendra raised her head. "I had two years of therapy," she continued doggedly, wanting to finish the story. "Then I went away to college. Ran away from college. I've been looking for myself ever since." She gave a short, bitter laugh. "I've never been able to have a serious relationship with any man, because it seems the only ones I meet have this fixation with guns. When they find I don't share their enthusiasm, they can't get away fast enough."

"And Jared—" SueAnn began.

"—is worse than all the rest," Kendra finished for her.

SueAnn shook her head. "I wasn't going to say that. Jared doesn't like guns. He probably hates them. But they are necessary tools of the trade."

"A trade he gave up five years ago," Kendra reminded.

SueAnn sighed. "You are one hard case. Let me put it another way. Jared had a knack for what he did in Special Forces. Do you know how many people try and fail to make it through the training? Do you suppose a surgeon would refuse to use his skills to save a life even after retiring from practice? No more can Jared turn his back on a situation such as we faced yesterday. He doesn't like it. He doesn't want to play hero. He simply does what has to be done."

"There you are!" Phil said in relief. "Didn't you hear Jared's page? We need to meet him at gate forty-eight."

SueAnn glanced around. "And we're at three!" Before anyone could blink, she stepped in front of an empty golf cart, forcing the driver to stop. "Gate forty-eight on the double!" She pressed a bill into the driver's hand.

Kendra began to laugh as she tossed her bags into the cart.

"What's so funny?" Phil asked beside her.

"*A woman who knows how to take charge and make things happen,*" Kendra said, with a glance at SueAnn. She looked back at Phil. "Watch you step, my friend!" She stepped into the car.

When they were seated, Phil looked at Kendra with a wink. "*Always,*" he said, slipping an arm around SueAnn.

The cart pulled to a stop and Jared reached up to help SueAnn with her bag. He noticed that the three were laughing and wondered what the joke was. He dared a glance at Kendra to find her smiling. He looked at Phil.

"Well," he drawled, "I hope it doesn't dampen your spirits any to hear the only seats I could get were in the pit."

"The pit?" Kendra asked.

Phil and SueAnn glanced at each other and shrugged. "No problem here," Phil said.

Jared looked at Kendra. "You don't know what the pit is?"

She shook her head.

"Then you don't have a problem, either. Come on. They're holding boarding for us." He caught up the bag Kendra had gotten out of storage.

"The good news is," Jared added as they hurried onboard the plane, "that we have the whole pit. There's room to stretch out if anyone wants to try and sleep."

"I have a problem sitting backwards," Phil said as he strapped himself into a forward facing seat. SueAnn immediately claimed the seat beside him.

Jared grinned. "I plan to be asleep before we are in the air, so I can sit anywhere. What about you, Kendra? There's still a seat by SueAnn."

"No, I—I'll try sitting backwards. I'm not a very good flier. Maybe that will help."

"Window or aisle?"

"Aisle, please."

Jared grabbed a pillow from the overhead storage and stepped over Phil's legs to the window seat. He strapped himself in and gave the flight attendant a thumbs up. She smiled and hurried away to prepare for takeoff.

Jared looked over to see SueAnn already asleep on Phil's shoulder, his blond head resting against her bright red curls. He grinned. His friend was truly and completely smitten.

He felt Kendra's gaze and looked up. She nodded toward the couple facing them. "They make a nice couple," she said, her voice low. "I just hope Phil is ready for her. She won't take no for an answer."

Jared adjusted his pillow, stretched out his legs beneath the empty seat across from him. "Well," he said, "I've known guys to have worse problems." With a final glance at her, he turned away and closed his eyes.

Kendra slowly unclenched her fists, feeling her cheeks burn with humiliation. How did one go about saying they were sorry and ask for another chance? Was it too late? She had chosen the neutral subject of Phil and SueAnn to try and break the ice and Jared had turned her words back on her.

Jared looked too sexy for words. The flight attendant had obviously been impressed. Somehow he had managed to change into a white knit polo shirt, the disreputable T-shirt no where in sight. The shirt stood out in stark contrast to his deep tan and black hair. Kendra found it hard to keep her eyes off him.

Kendra shifted in the uncomfortable seat, realizing that it did not recline. She couldn't stretch out her legs without kicking Phil who sat directly across from her. She looked longingly at the seat beside Jared, at his shoulder where she could be resting her head as SueAnn did with Phil. Her mouth twisted. No one would ever accuse her of being someone who took charge and made things happen. She leaned back and closed her eyes.

Jared looked up as SueAnn touched his knee. She beckoned for him to lean forward and caught his hands as he did.

She put her mouth close to his ear and whispered, then squeezed his hands and returned to Phil's shoulder. Before closing her eyes, she gave him a wink of encouragement.

Jared sat back and mulled over SueAnn's words. "Be patient with Kendra," she'd said. "She's gonna take a lot of work. She has a good reason to hate guns. Trust me. I'll explain later. Oh, and remember what she said about being a bad flier? Maybe you could hold her hand, or something!"

He glanced over to see Kendra with her hands clenched tightly together. Her eyes were closed.

"Are you all right?" he asked.

She looked at him. "Why do you ask?"

"You said you were a bad flier? Does that mean you're afraid?"

She shrugged. "I just don't like it much. I'm okay."

"You might be more comfortable over here. You'd have more room to stretch out."

"I'm fine," she said, sounding a little breathless.

"Well, I'm not!" He leaned over and unsnapped her seat belt. "You're too far away!" He pulled her across the distance until she sat beside him. He began looking for her seat belt.

"I can do that!" Kendra pushed his hands away.

"Is everything all right?" The flight attendant appeared beside them.

"It is now," Jared assured her, hearing Kendra's seat belt click shut.

"Good." The girl's smile was more forced this time. "We're next in line for takeoff. Try to stay seated."

"Will do."

Jared touched Kendra's hand. "If you need something to hang onto during takeoff, I'm here."

She looked at him. "Thanks. I don't generally get too hysterical."

He grinned. "This could get a little bumpy."

He heard a hitch in her breath. "What do you mean?"

Jared pointed out the window. "See those clouds. If we aren't in the air in about ten minutes, we're going to sit here awhile. And if we are in the air, we might feel a few gusts from that thunderstorm."

Kendra shivered. "I've flown through storms before."

"When?"

"Coming back from Kuwait."

Jared fell silent.

"I don't think I ever got to say thanks—"

"Don't. It was my job."

"Of course. But it was a lot more than that to me." She leaned her head back against the seat and Jared saw her swallow. Her lashes fluttered against her cheeks and he saw that they were spiked with tears.

Without thinking, Jared reached for her hand, capturing it in both of his, gently stroking her wrist with his thumb. He looked up to find her gaze on him, her gray eyes wide with pain and confusion. He felt his heart twist at the thought that he might be the cause of her turmoil.

He lifted the armrest to pull her closer, cradle her against him.

"Don't write me off just yet, Kendra! Give me a chance to make things right between us. Whatever I've done, I'm sorry."

"Oh, Jared, it isn't you. I've never been any good at relationships. It's all my fault. I let my expectations exceed reality."

"Your expectations should exceed reality. How else can you grow?"

"I haven't done any growing for at least twelve years. My life has been on perpetual hold."

"Maybe it's time to make some changes," Jared suggested.

"No doubt about that!" She shrugged. "There's just some things you can't get beyond, no matter how hard you try."

This probably wasn't the time, and maybe not the place, but Jared saw an opening and went for it."

"Such as your hating guns?"

Kendra tensed as if an electric current had touched her. Then she slumped against the seat. "A perfect example."

A sudden gust of wind from the approaching storm rocked the plane and Kendra clutched at Jared's shirt. He put his hand over hers and pressed it against his chest.

"Relax. Better down here than in the air."

She shivered. "This is just like Kuwait."

Jared shook his head and drew her closer. "No. You didn't have me beside you in Kuwait."

CHAPTER FIVE

Jared and Phil were on their second cup of coffee when SueAnn joined them in the hotel dining room the next morning.

"Kendra was spirited away by her boss a couple of hours ago—some three star general," she announced, spooning sugar into her coffee. "*Geez!* She works for the DIA, the *Defense Intelligence Agency*. Why didn't you guys tell me?" She glanced from one to the other.

Phil looked at Jared. "Did you know?"

Jared had tensed and then slumped forward, a frown creasing his brow. "Actually, I did. I just didn't realize that I knew."

"Say again."

"Remember Kuwait, when we brought out those operatives?"

Phil drew in his breath. "That—was Kendra?"

"Yeah."

Phil shook his head. "I guess the disguise worked. It fooled me."

"Me too," Jared said.

"What are you two talking about?" SueAnn sipped her coffee, winced.

"Knowing the Iraqis were on the way, Kendra's team leader insisted she dress in men's clothing and cut her hair. With her voice, she apparently was able to fool them, as well as us. We saw a scraggly kid, too young to even have a beard. They were all pretty dirty and had been roughed up a bit." Jared's jaw tightened. "She had a black eye, as I remember."

"Yeah," Phil said darkly, cradling his coffee. "And a busted lip."

"Jared, there's something you have to know," SueAnn said, playing with her napkin. "I may not have another chance to tell you."

He looked at her. "About Kendra and guns?"

"That's right."

"Well?" Jared said, a moment later, when SueAnn did not speak.

She swallowed. "This isn't easy. It's not like I'm betraying a confidence. It's just very hard to talk about."

"Take your time." Jared watched her.

She drew a deep breath. "Yesterday she told me that when she was sixteen she was babysitting her nine year old brother and a neighbor at the neighbor's home. While the boys were playing in a bedroom, her brother blew his head off with a gun they found. Even after years of therapy, she still hasn't forgiven herself."

Jared put down his cup and raked a hand through his hair. "That's a good reason to hate guns, all right." He felt as if a giant fist squeezed his heart, killing all feeling, bringing blessed numbness. He stood.

"Jared, where are you going?" SueAnn asked in concern.

He made a vague gesture. "Is there some reason to hang around?"

"A very good one. Named Kendra, remember?"

"SueAnn, I know you mean well, but I'm not man enough to deal with that kind of emotional baggage—"

"You're the only man who can."

He shook his head. "I'm afraid you greatly overestimate me. As Kendra pointed out a couple of days ago, I've lost my edge since I left the army. Sorry to disappoint you."

SueAnn's lip curled. "Disappointment doesn't begin to describe my feelings. *Contempt* comes a lot closer."

Jared gave a mock bow. *"My lady."* He turned and walked from the room. He could feel SueAnn staring at him all the way out the door.

Jared did not stop walking until he found himself by the reflecting pool in front of the Washington Monument. He was still there two hours later when Phil walked up beside him.

"How's it going?" Jared asked, looking up at his friend.

"I was about to ask you that, but I can see the answer on your face." Phil dropped to the bench beside him, tossed popcorn to a trio of pigeons.

"I suppose you have some advice to offer?" Jared said.

"Nope. They dragged SueAnn off about an hour ago. I'm just looking for some place to hang out for the next few hours."

"How did we ever get involved with a pair like those two?"

Phil crossed one ankle over his knee. "Because we're so jaded most women bore us to tears. Kendra and SueAnn are different. They're in charge of their lives. They make things happen. For my part, I don't intend to let either of them go, regardless of a bit of baggage."

Jared looked at him. "What do you have in mind?"

"Well, they're good for each other. They aren't that comfortable with other women. What do they have in common with them, for crying out loud?" Phil cleared his throat. "Anyway, I think SueAnn can help Kendra. She's a psychologist, after all. And I'll be there for both of them."

"I wish you luck," Jared said. "You're a better man than me."

Phil looked at him, shook his head. "And to think that for as long as I've known you, I've envied you. I didn't think you were afraid of anything."

Jared shrugged. "So now you know. Get over it."

Phil stood, scattering the rest of the popcorn for the pigeons. He watched the birds scrabbling for the food.

"You know, you could learn from these birds," Phil said.

Jared shot him a quizzical glance. "I could?"

"Some things in life are gifts and not to be questioned. You should simply grab onto them for all you're worth." He threw the crumpled bag into a trash can. "The next guy might not have a bag of popcorn." He strode away, hands in his pockets, whistling a jaunty tune.

Jared sat for a moment, a slow grin twisting his mouth. Phil might not be the world's greatest philosopher, but every once in a while he came up with a gem worth consideration.

"I'll see you guys later," Kendra said. "Thanks for dinner—and the company!" She inserted her key card into the door, pushed it open and dropped her briefcase in the hall.

The sound of someone clearing their throat brought her up short. She paused in the act of peeling off her jacket to peer around the corner.

"You might not want to go any further with that," Jared drawled, quirking a brow. He lounged on the bed, pillows stacked against the headboard.

Kendra froze for a moment before shrugging back into her jacket. She reached up to pull a clasp from her hair, which fell of its own weight to cascade around her shoulders.

"What are you doing here?"

"I couldn't leave without you."

She sat down at the desk, watching him in the mirror. "That's not what I heard." *Why did he have to look so desirable, and as if he belonged in her bed!*

Jared sat up and swung his feet to the floor. "I had to do some thinking, decide if—"

"You don't have to explain anything, Jared. Believe me, I understand. You're right, you know."

His eyes met and held hers in the mirror. "*What* do you understand, and *why* am I right?"

"I know SueAnn told you why I have—this thing about guns. And you're right that you can't help me. If anyone could have helped, I'm sure it would have happened a long time ago."

Jared paced a few steps. "I'm curious about one thing. How did you ever get past the psychologists in Army Intelligence?"

Kendra shrugged. "When I ran away from college and joined the army, I didn't have anything to live for. That meant that I wasn't afraid of anything. That can be a useful attribute in the right place—and I found that place."

"But you still had to learn to handle guns?"

"I didn't have a problem with big guns, and I was really good with the self-defense training. Somehow I faked my way through."

He raked a hand through his hair. "And all of this to atone for—" he broke off, swallowed. "Kendra, I can help you. I know I can."

She laughed, deep and throaty, with tears just below the surface. "Why would you want to?"

"Because I've never met anyone like you."

"I've never met anyone like me, either." Kendra stood with a dismissive gesture. "Well, maybe your luck will hold, and you'll never meet anyone else like me."

"I've had all the luck I need in meeting you," Jared said, his voice low and persuasive. "Come with me, Kendra."

Her eyes widened. "Come with you? Where, pray tell? I've already had dinner, and I don't feel like dancing."

"Who said anything about dancing? I have a cabin in Colorado, just north of Denver. I want to take you there and let you finish the expedition, one on one."

Kendra stared at him, made an impatient movement with her head. "To what end?"

"You paid for the program. When do you report for duty?"

"Not for a few weeks."

"I told you we can tailor programs for particular needs, to overcome certain fears, for instance. I want to design one for you."

She pressed her lips together, licked them. "And what does that require of me? That I learn to shoot a handgun?" This last flippantly.

"Among other things," Jared said, watching her.

Kendra felt the blood drain from her face until her skin tingled. She put out a hand for support.

"I can't—I can't even bear to think of touching a handgun, let alone actually using one." She looked at Jared. "Save yourself the time and frustration. I told you that you can't help me." Her voice reflected bitterness and defeat.

Jared walked over to stand close enough to touch. His gaze captured hers. "Kendra, do you want to be whole again?"

She laughed, the sound dry and brittle. She turned away from him. "What difference does it make? Why does it matter?"

He caught her shoulders. "It matters because your fears—your *hangups*, if you will—are keeping you from accepting me and my world. I want you in my world, Kendra. I've never been more certain of anything."

Jared looked down into her eyes, saw hope lose out to disbelief, then her eyes pooled with tears. Her shoulders sagged.

"Jared, I can't!"

"Shhhhh!" He drew her close, cradled her against him. "Don't answer tonight. Think about it. I'm just next door." He put her away from him, wondering if he had ever done anything in his life as hard as letting her go. "If your answer is still no in the morning, I'll be on the next flight back to Denver, and you'll never see me again."

She drew a sobbing breath. "You—think that's what I want?"

"Are there other choices, Kendra? I won't stay around and cause you pain. If I can't help you, I'll get out of your life."

"Just like that? You make it sound—so clinical."

"Not just like that. I've—"

"Do you know I've dreamed of meeting you for ten years?" She raised her eyes to his, wet her lips.

Jared stared. "How? I don't understand."

"You might not have realized I was a woman when you rescued us in Kuwait, but I knew you were a man, the only one to ever touch my soul. Since then, every man I've met has come in a poor second. I had almost begun to believe you were a fantasy—someone I had conjured up. Then, wonder of wonders, you show up as leader of my expedition. Only that didn't turn out so well—"

"I'm offering to make it up to you," Jared said.

A smile touched her lips. "It's very tempting."

Jared turned away. "Sleep on it. We'll talk in the morning—before I leave."

"Before you leave?"

He paused with his hand on the door between their rooms. "Before I leave, Kendra, either *with* you, or *without* you." He stepped into his room and closed the door.

Jared stood leaning against the door, breathing as if he had just run five miles. He slowly straightened and moved across the room to drop into a chair.

He remembered that night, the scrawny kid with the dark hair and huge gray eyes, and the longest lashes he'd ever seen. It all made sense now. How could he not have realized he was looking at a woman? A girl, he corrected. Kendra would have been barely twenty then.

A smile touched his lips. *She had changed a bit.* He doubted she could pull off the same deception now. She was all healthy, desirable woman.

His smile faded. If she agreed to his plan, that would not be part of the agenda. He had to help her, not seduce her.

Even if she was the first woman in a long time to touch his soul.

Was he as jaded as Phil implied? He hadn't felt jaded since meeting Kendra. He felt alive, expectant. The self-sufficient and capable Kendra Allen might be able to bring low all the world's most vicious criminals. But beneath that tough façade lurked a little girl still afraid of the dark. He had to teach her that darkness was good and held its own wonders, or else she would never be able to appreciate the light.

Kendra stood at her window, staring out at the moonlight. There was nothing to keep her from going with Jared, from completing the expedition. *Nothing except her own fear of failure.* Long ago she had learned her limitations and knew what to expect of herself. She did not get into situations where she did not have control. She had also not pushed herself in a very long time. Was it time to challenge the boundaries she had set for herself? *To find out if she could indeed be a whole person for the first time in her adult life.*

She thought of Jared lying on her bed, his shirt open halfway down his chest, the look in his eyes as she had started to remove her jacket. That look had held admiration and desire and iron control. He said he wanted her in his world. God knows, she wanted him in hers! Dare she risk failure when the cost would be the one thing in life she couldn't live without? There was no choice to make. If she didn't risk it, she had already lost him.

Phil caught Kendra in a warm embrace. "You're going to be all right, sweetheart," he reassured her. "You know that don't you? Jared won't let anything happen to you."

64

Kendra looked into his concerned blue eyes, glanced over to where Jared and SueAnn were deep in conversation.

"I'm not worried about Jared, Phil." She looked back at him. "You know my problem. I'm just afraid—that he won't be able to help me, either."

He caught her hands and squeezed them. "Whatever happens, you keep in touch, all right?" He released her as Jared and SueAnn joined them.

"Sure thing," Kendra said, looking up at Jared.

"My turn," SueAnn said as she slid an arm around Kendra's shoulders and led her a few steps away. "I wish I could give you some advice that you haven't already heard a thousand times. I know you're doing the right thing. And I know you have already figured this out, but Jared is a one in a million kinda guy. You have a lot at stake. Don't lose him, Kendra."

Kendra looked at SueAnn and wished again that she had met her sooner. Unable to speak, she caught her in a wordless embrace, blinking away a sheen of tears.

"Promise me something," SueAnn said, holding her away. "Keep in touch, whatever happens?"

Kendra laughed through her tears. "Do you and Phil rehearse these things, or do you really think that much alike?"

SueAnn joined in the laughter as they turned back to the men. Jared and Phil shook hands, promising to see each other in a couple of weeks. Then Jared took Kendra's arm and hurried her over to the gate where boarding was already in progress.

Kendra settled into a seat by the window, wondering if the silent treatment was part of Jared's program. He had barely spoken two words to her since she had walked into his room this morning after a sleepless night and announced that she would go with him.

Maybe she should have waited for him to ask, Kendra realized now. Maybe he had changed his mind during the night and no longer wanted her. But she had been so afraid of exactly that, that she hadn't been willing to take any chance on being left behind. When he opened his eyes this morning, she had been sitting on the side of his bed, waiting for him to wake up.

She had indulged in all sorts of fantasies as she watched him sleep. The white sheets had been in sharp contrast to his bronzed skin and black hair. One out flung arm rested on top of the covers and she could see a silver chain around his neck, disappearing into the dark hairs on his chest.

She stole a glance at him now. Movie star handsome, she wondered momentarily why he hadn't become a stuntman or actor, then realized that was exactly what he was doing with his company, *Extreme Expeditions*, or Double E, as everyone seemed to shorten it. If you were willing to pay the price, you could star in your own real life version of whatever struck your fancy. From the literature a friend had given her, she knew the programs Jared and his crew designed were gaining in popularity, even to the point of Fortune 500 companies sending their top executives. How, then, did she rate her very own instructor and her very own program?

Jared glanced at Kendra as she stared out the window. She wore her hair loose this morning, the first time he had seen it that way, aside from last night. A rich brown, it fell around her shoulders and partially hid her face, concealing her exquisite bone structure.

He almost groaned as he remembered waking this morning to find her sitting on his bed waiting for him to wake up. Only years of rigid control kept him from dragging her down on the bed and kissing her senseless. Instead, he had listened to her tell him that she had decided to go with him and continue the program he chose. Then he had curtly ordered her back to her room so he

66

could get dressed, when what he really wanted to do was shout his joy that she cared enough to try.

He looked at Kendra again and felt his lips twitch. He could almost feel sorry for what he intended to put her through. The only thing that kept that emotion in check was the knowledge that he would be suffering every bit as much as she did. Until this morning, he had honestly believed that he would be able to resist the temptation she presented. Now he knew that one Kendra Allen was about to test all the control he had mustered during years of the most strenuous training the human body could endure.

He momentarily thought of the Garden of Eden and felt acute sympathy for Adam. Not until this moment could he fully relate to Adam's weakness and mankind's downfall.

CHAPTER SIX

Kendra threw her bags into the back of the Jeep that had been left at the Denver airport for Jared. They would continue the rest of the way by vehicle. Jared had decided against having Mark take them in by helicopter, feeling that they would be too isolated in case something happened. Now he looked at her.

"Can you drive a five-speed?"

She nodded.

"Four wheel drive?"

Another nod.

He tossed her the keys. "Show me. I have to know you can handle it. If you can't, that will be the first lesson."

She shrugged. *"You're the boss."* She climbed behind the wheel.

"Enough already!" Ten minutes and fifteen miles later, Jared threw up his hands. "Pull over."

Kendra complied, throwing him an innocent look. "Is there a problem?"

"Just that you're enjoying this too much. I'd prefer to get there in one piece." He climbed out. "Move over."

"You didn't ask how I knew how to drive off-road vehicles?" Kendra said a few minutes later when they were back on the road.

"I assume the military."

"At first, yes. But I liked it so much that I bought my own SUV and spend a lot of my time off with a group of four-wheel enthusiasts. I've toured a great deal of the country that way."

"Don't you know these things can be dangerous?" he growled.

"You're forgetting a vital piece of information I gave you last night."

"I didn't forget. *You aren't afraid of anything.* Except handguns, that is."

Kendra drew a sharp breath. "That's about it."

Jared reached over and pushed a button on the console. A few seconds later, music filled the air.

"Desperation?" Kendra named a popular musical group, trying and failing to keep the astonishment from her voice.

He slanted a glance at her. "I like them. Is that all right with you?"

"Well, yeah. Of course. They just happen to be my favorite group. I especially like to play *Final Flight* when I drive in an off-road rally."

Jared muttered something under his breath. Kendra ignored him and hummed along with a couple of songs.

As introductory music for the next song filled the air, Jared reached over and turned off the CD player.

"Hey! That one's my favorite. I sometimes put my CD on continuous play and just listen to that song all day."

"Not right now," Jared grated. "That song is a bit too descriptive for me to handle at the moment."

Kendra hummed a few words, threw him a look, and lapsed into a thoughtful silence.

"Snow bound in love... What more could I want... What more could I dream than to be snowbound in love with you." Pretty vivid, all right. A smile tugged at her lips.

Was it possible the Major wasn't as much in control as he wanted her to believe?

"Can you talk about your brother's death, Kendra?" Jared said abruptly. "Tell me everything that happened to you afterward. SueAnn thinks that's a good place for us to start."

Kendra jerked upright in her seat, hands gripping the sides of the cushion. "Oh, God!" she whispered.

"Take your time. We're still about ten minutes from the cabin. Just tell it your way."

She put her hands over her face, felt them trembling. Her whole body shook with remembered horror.

"Kendra, you have to do this. Make me understand. I know these fears are perfectly logical in your mind. That's where we have to start."

"Bobby was nine," she said, her voice dull and void of expression. "Blond, blue eyes. A perfect child. I babysat him a lot and never had any trouble with him. He hadn't been feeling well for awhile and I was becoming concerned. He never seemed to want to play.

"This particular night, my parents went out to dinner with our neighbors. They had an eight year old son named Timmy. He was Bobby's best friend. I had sat for both of them many times since I was twelve. Maybe that was the problem. I trusted them too much.

"They watched television for a while and then said they wanted to go play in Timmy's room. I had homework to do, so I sat at the kitchen table and opened my books.

"About ten minutes later, I heard a shot and Timmy scream. I don't remember moving, but I was beside Bobby, gathering him in my arms, picking up a piece of his skull in my hand. His blood was everywhere. I didn't do anything, just went into shock, I guess. I learned later that Timmy called his parents at the restaurant and they called an ambulance. When they got there, I hadn't moved, just sat there holding Bobby.

"When they took him away from me, and pried his skull out of my hand, I began screaming. I screamed until I couldn't make a sound, then I kept trying to scream. They put me in a straight jacket and a padded cell. I didn't eat, so they fed me with IV's.

"I didn't speak for a month, and when I did my voice was barely a croak. It took a year for it to improve to where it is now and it never got any better. I figure this is my curse, a constant reminder of what I let happen."

Kendra stopped speaking, unknotted her hands from one another, and raised her head. The Jeep had come to a stop in front of a small cabin. She couldn't look at Jared.

"Is this it?" she asked, trying to sound flippant, but barely managing a husky whisper. "The place where I come to terms with my destiny."

"This is my cabin," Jared said. "Kendra, look at me."

She opened the door and stepped out. "I can't."

71

She heard Jared's door open and felt him beside her. "Kendra, you didn't let it happen. It wasn't your fault." His quiet voice washed over her.

She sighed. "You don't know how much I would like to believe that, but I was in charge. I was supposed to be taking care of them."

"Where did the gun come from?"

"You know, that's the most criminal thing of all. Mr. Matthews, Timmy's father, had received a trunk of mementos from an uncle who had passed away. The aunt had just thrown in a bunch of things she thought he might want, and shipped it to him. He had opened it and glanced through it, but didn't see anything of much importance. Timmy was excited about it, however, so Mr. Matthews put it in his room until he had a chance to go through it. Timmy thought it was a treasure chest. I remember him asking Bobby if he wanted to go play pirates.

"Mr. Matthews was devastated. He had no idea the gun was in the trunk. His aunt was in her late seventies and fairly senile. From what he could get from her, she thought it was a toy gun and had thrown it in for Timmy. It turned out to be his uncle's service revolver."

"What about your parent's, Kendra?"

She turned away. "What about them?"

"Did they blame you?"

"No. It would have been easier if they had."

"Why do you say that?"

"They were so concerned about me, that I had gone so totally off the deep end. They had already lost Bobby and didn't know what was going to happen to me. I never really let them properly grieve for him." She reached up and raked her fingers through her hair, pushing it back from her face.

"When I was coherent again, able to recognize things, and saw my mother, her hair had turned from dark brown to completely white. She was only thirty seven." Kendra turned to look at Jared. "*I did that to her.* Another reminder of my guilt."

She reached into the Jeep and picked up her bag. "Shall we? Whatever you have in mind, let's get started. Unless you've decided I was right, after all. *That there's no hope for me.*"

Jared stood looking down at Kendra as she stared defiantly back at him. He wanted to touch her, hold her, comfort her, kiss away all the hurt. He could do none of that. One of the goals he had set for himself was not to put any kind of personal pressure on her. There would be time for that later, once she overcame the fear and guilt that had controlled almost half her life.

"What do you want to do right now?" he asked. "Rest for a while?"

She shook her head. "A five mile run over rugged terrain sounds more like it. I need action. I don't want to think!"

"Fine. We'll change—"

"I want to go alone."

He had turned away and now swung back to face her.

"No, Kendra. There have been cougar sightings up here recently. You will not go anywhere away from the cabin without me."

Her eyes flashed in disbelief. "You're just telling me that!"

"No. I wouldn't do that. You have to trust me, Kendra. If I tell you to do something, you will obey. It could be a matter of life and death."

She moved to pass him. "I know about life and death." Her voice was so dry it threatened to crack.

Jared's hand shot out, and then she was in his arms. He kissed her hair, stroked her back, murmured soothing words.

"I will help you, Kendra. I promise! I can't watch you suffer like this."

"Hey!" she tried to joke. "I'm used to it. Kind of like the grain of sand to the oyster." But the eyes she raised to his swam with tears.

He grinned, brushed away a tear with his thumb. "You're something else, you know."

"I think we've been there." She moved away from him. "Why are you doing this?"

"I think we've been there." He reached inside the Jeep for his bag. "We'll bring the rest in later. A run sounds good." He fished a key out of his pocket and tossed it to her, noting with satisfaction that she caught it with one hand. "That's for the cabin. Remind me to give you the spare for the Jeep."

"Why?"

"Sometimes things happen, Kendra. There's no phone up here, so I need to show you how to use the radio, too."

"I think I should be able to manage that," she said.

"That's right. You probably already know. It is military issue."

She paused on the steps, looking down at him. "You bring me up here where you imply there might be things out of your control. What exactly do you have in mind with this project?"

"We both know there are things out of our control. I might plunge off a cliff and you would be up here alone. I want you to know how to call Mark or Phil. I might break a leg. It would be nice if you could get me back to civilization, or at least call for help. Other than that, I intend to keep you too busy to think."

She held his gaze for a moment, nodded. "Sounds good to me." She turned and stuck her key in the lock. "In case it's important, I don't cook."

He reached around her and pushed the door open. *"Then you'll learn."* He made a sweeping gesture for her to precede him into the cabin and grinned as he heard her grinding her teeth.

Kendra flopped down on the steps and watched as Jared jogged the last few yards. Perfectly toned muscles strained and flexed. Sweat glistened on his skin and soaked the ragged T-shirt he had pulled on over jogging shorts. She had hoped the run would take the edge off some of the tension she felt, but it had only made things worse. Watching such a prime male specimen in action had only served to tighten nerves already stretched past the breaking point.

Except to comfort, he had not touched her since he had seen her expression after she found his gun. Certainly there had been nothing to compare with those kisses on the trail when he finally realized she had not exaggerated the danger.

Kendra sighed. She wanted him to kiss her again. Wanted to feel his arms around her. She licked her lips. She had no idea how one would go about seducing a man with the kind of control Jared practiced as a matter of course. That was one task she would not set for herself. Better to focus on what he had in store for her.

She stood as he approached the porch. "I saw a waterfall a half mile back. Would it be okay to go for a dip?"

He threw her a wary glance.

"Please." She plucked at the sports bra, soaked and clinging to her chest. "I'm hot and sticky. A nice swim would be great."

"Don't go alone. I need to make a call."

"Then meet me there. What can happen in five minutes?"

Jared looked after her, deciding whether or not to let her go, then his radio crackled. He sighed as he reached for it. He couldn't watch her every second. *She probably needed the space as much as he did.*

Kendra floated on her back in the clear pool. The water felt perfect. She drew in a breath, closed her eyes and let herself sink to the bottom, something she had learned as a child and perfected over the years.

Kendra felt the tension drain from her body and knew it was time to come up. The serenity shattered as something hit the water above her with a thud. She expelled the last of her breath and shot to the surface.

"Kendra! Are you all right?" Jared grabbed her shoulders, shook her. "I saw you lying on the bottom—"

Kendra felt her teeth rattle. "I'm—fine. Or I will be if you'll stop shaking me!"

"What were you doing down there?"

"Just playing around. Holding my breath."

"You scared me to death!" His eyes blazed with anger—and more.

Kendra shrugged. "Sorry. I didn't know."

"Sorry doesn't cut it, sweetheart!"

She licked her lips. "I didn't mean to frighten you. I didn't think—"

"That's obvious! Is that what's wrong with you? You've held your breath for so long you've destroyed all your brain cells."

She stared at him, tried to move away. "I don't believe that is called for, Major. I've apologized. I don't think I'm responsible for your misguided sense of—what did you call it—*civic responsibility.*"

76

"Maybe not." His eyes burned into hers. *"But you can accept responsibility for this."* His hands moved to cup her face, pull it to his.

"No!" Kendra whispered. Moments ago, she would have died for his kiss, but not like this, not in this mood. "Please—"

His mouth cut off her words, and all coherent thought. She didn't bother to struggle. The hot blood that coursed through her seemed amplified by the cool water lapping around them. She could only clutch at his shoulders and move her mouth to answer his.

Jared raised his head and put Kendra away from him to hold her at arms length. *He was not supposed to touch her!* He would not confuse the issues with emotional involvement. His arms fell and he stepped back.

"Well, that was certainly fun." He hardly recognized his own voice, so harsh with control.

It took all the will power he could muster not to reach for her, to cradle her in his arms, to tell her how much he wanted her. But now was not the time. It would not be time until she stood before him as an equal. Suddenly daunted by the task he had set for himself, Jared turned away to climb out of the pool and pick up his shirt.

Kendra stiffened and felt the blood drain from her face. He had said she could accept responsibility for what happened, *but what had happened?* She had had no intention of seducing Jared—had not thought it possible.

Kendra raised her head. In spite of her emotional trauma, she could not take her eyes off Jared. He had the most perfect body she had ever seen. Just looking at him made her feel like melting. His touch set her afire. How would she endure the next two weeks?

Jared pulled the tattered shirt over his damp chest and drew a hand across his mouth. What had he been thinking? The body he had spent years getting in peak physical shape and kept that way as a tool of his trade now trembled like a leaf in a breeze. For a moment his hunger threatened to overwhelm him and he searched his innermost depths for the control that never deserted him. He sat down on a rock to put on his shoes and tried to ignore the fine tremor in his fingers.

Jared stood and picked up Kendra's shirt. "Come on out before you freeze to death. I'll let you have the warm water tonight."

She emerged from the water and he held the shirt as she slipped her arms into it. She pulled it close around her.

"What do you mean?" she asked. "About the warm water?"

"There's a small solar collector that heats a few gallons. Warm only, mind you."

"Warm sounds wonderful." She pulled on her socks and stuck her feet into her shoes.

"Here, let me." Jared saw her hands shaking and knelt to tie her shoes.

"How does—why did it get so cold so quickly?" Her teeth were chattering and Kendra wrapped her arms around herself for warmth.

He grinned. "The sun went down. That happens fast at this elevation." He caught her hand and pulled her to her feet. "Come on. We need to get back."

CHAPTER SEVEN

"I won't make you cook tonight," Jared said as he pushed open the door. "There are sandwiches in the cooler. Take a shower and get some dry clothes on while I bring in our dinner. You should find a couple of towels and a robe in the bathroom."

Jared quickly stripped off his own wet clothes and put on jeans and a sweatshirt. He bent to touch a match to the wood and kindling already in the fireplace. As he straightened he heard a shriek and a muffled exclamation from the bathroom. He grinned. Kendra had used up all the warm water. He pulled open the door to bring in their gear.

When he returned, Kendra sat on the hearth, pulling a comb through her damp hair. She wore jeans and a flannel shirt with several of the top buttons still open.

She looked at him, a smile playing around her mouth. "You weren't exaggerating when you said there were only a few gallons of warm water!"

He did not return her smile. "I told you I don't exaggerate about anything. Before we go any further, I guess we need to establish whether or not you intend to keep challenging me, or will you grant me your trust?"

She looked up and the depth of pain in her eyes staggered him. She stood, dropping the comb on a table, and jammed her hands in the pockets of her jeans. He saw her lick her lips.

"Jared, this isn't personal." The degree of huskiness in her voice had increased. "Trust is something that disappeared from my life when my brother's body was torn out of my arms. It isn't a matter of not wanting to trust you. It's a matter of not being able to trust anyone or anything." She raised troubled gray eyes to his. "Can you understand that at all?"

He didn't answer. "How do you go on a mission without trust in the other operatives?" he asked instead.

"They're highly trained, as am I. I *know* they will do their jobs."

"You *trust* them to do their jobs," he said.

"That isn't trust. It's confidence based on previous experience."

"And how do you define trust?" Jared asked, watching her, feeling her pain and confusion.

"As hope. Expectations. To be able to rely on things like honesty, integrity, and justice."

Jared heard his own bitter laugh. *"In today's world?"* He raked a hand through his hair. "So, without previous experience, you have no confidence that I can do my job." He whirled back to face her. "It's your call, Kendra. I can ask Mark to pick you up in the morning. Without your trust, I can't proceed. I will be putting both our lives in danger."

She looked at him. "Pick me up? What will you do?"

He looked around the cabin. "Stay here. This is where I come to lick my wounds. I'm due a few days off."

"Could I—" she broke off, raking a hand through her wet hair, pushing it back from her face.

"No," Jared said. "You can't."

Her head jerked up. "How do—"

"You want to know if you can just stay here, too. Forget about the program. I can't let you do that."

She caught her bottom lip between her teeth. "Why not?"

"Because then you would have no reason to trust me. I didn't bring you up here to seduce you, Kendra," he added with brutal frankness.

Her face flamed. "Yeah, well, I can see where you wouldn't see any challenge in that!" She turned away and he could see her trembling.

"Kendra," Jared swallowed. "What we do to each other could be dangerous, in more ways than one, until we know where this is going."

"Where *what* is going?" she asked, tensing.

He shrugged, although she still had her back to him. *"This relationship. This attraction.* Call it whatever you like. Where do you see it going?"

"How would I know?" Her laugh was bitter. "I've never had one."

Jared started. "Would you please repeat that?"

She turned to face him, humiliation evident in her eyes. "I've never had a relationship before. I've never even had a date."

"Now that I don't believe," Jared drawled with feigned casualness.

"Why would I lie about something like that? Why would I admit it unless it's true?"

"And would you care to explain something that can be nothing short of phenomenal? How can you possibly never have had a date? A relationship? Maybe I can buy that, but a date?"

"I was a very immature sixteen-year-old. I competed in a lot of sports. I was actually training for the Olympics, so I wouldn't have had time to date anyway." She went back to sit before the hearth, running her fingers through her hair. "The next three years, I hardly remember. All my time seemed to be spent with shrinks, until I ran away and joined the Army."

"Then what?"

"Well, first off, most of the guys thought I was gay, else why was I there. That suited me fine. I concentrated literally on being the best that I could be. I found a niche and excelled.

"Later, when I might have been interested in men, I found that a woman who knows a dozen ways to kill with her bare hands doesn't top anyone's list as their idea of a fun date."

Jared couldn't help it. His lips twitched. "That just happens to come up in casual conversation, does it?"

She glanced up, eyes accusing. "You're laughing at me."

He couldn't deny it. "Maybe. I'll admit you are intimidating. We talked about that."

She shrugged. "So maybe that's the problem. What kind of woman is interested in a man she intimidates?"

"Suppose you tell me."

She faced him, her eyes snapping. "I do not intimidate you, Major. We did talk about that. I didn't believe you then, and I don't believe you now. I know the signs. When I found you in my hotel room, I had my answer."

82

He shrugged. "Okay, let's say I'm not intimidated. That might be enough to pique your interest. It isn't enough to hold it."

"Wanna bet?" She made an attempt at a smile. "Do you know how rare that is?"

"You told me. That's still not an answer. In fact, do you have one?"

She looked puzzled. "Do I have what?"

"An answer?"

"To what question?"

"Does one really want a mercenary?"

Kendra stared at him as color washed into her face. After a moment she turned away without speaking.

"I see that you do." Jared's voice was carefully measured. "And very eloquently stated, at that."

She whirled back to face him. "No. *You don't understand.*"

"I understand all too well, Kendra. I know very well what I am and what women think of me. It's all the rage to be able to tell their friends that they made it with someone like me. But they would never dream of taking me home to meet their family, into polite society, or to the office party."

"That's not true!" Kendra whispered. "You have so much to offer."

His shoulders slumped. "I have nothing to offer, Kendra. I don't even know if I have any humanity left. If so, I'm down to the bitter dregs."

"Jared, you have more humanity left that most people ever start out with. Why are you saying these things? Are you trying to scare me away?"

When he did not answer, Kendra looked up.

"Yes," Jared said.

"Why?" she asked, drawing a startled breath.

"Because that's easier than admitting how scared I am." He held her gaze for a moment then turned and walked out of the cabin.

Kendra stood frozen, staring after Jared. Apparently what happened at the waterfall had affected him as deeply as it had her. *But differently.* She wanted more and he was running scared. A man who wasn't afraid of anything, except what she made him feel.

She had to back off, Kendra realized. Would she take him up on his offer to leave? *Not a chance.* Whether he could help her or not, whether or not his program worked, she had to see it through or lose him forever. The last was unthinkable.

Did she trust him? She didn't even have to think about it. *Unconditionally.*

The door opened and Jared came in with a couple of bags from the Jeep. Kendra hurried to help him.

Jared stopped, held her gaze. "Have you decided?" His voice was neutral, his expression masked.

"Yes."

"And?"

"I'm staying."

He put the bags on the table before speaking again. "Why?" *Just the one word.*

Kendra's answer was just as simple. "I have to."

He turned, trapped her in his gaze, and for a moment she saw his own pain and vulnerability. In that moment she knew that in his own way, he was as wounded as she. He looked away.

"Let's eat," he growled. "And throw some more wood on the fire, will you? We'll eat over there. It's a bit warmer."

While Kendra tended the fire, Jared carried over a low table and set it on the rug in front of the hearth. He went back to return with a tray of sandwiches from a well known deli chain and a couple of soft drinks.

"My kind of food," Kendra grinned, digging in without an invitation.

"Enjoy it now. Tomorrow night we run a cold camp."

"Cold camp?"

"No fire. That means the civilian equivalent of MREs."

"We'll be gone overnight?"

"We'll be gone for two nights."

"And our destination?"

"We're going to climb the peak you can see to the northwest." Jared threw her a glance. "Nothing builds trust quite like scaling a cliff."

Kendra's hand trembled and she swallowed carefully, the sandwich she had been enjoying suddenly tasting like sawdust.

"I—" She put down her plate and wiped her hands down her jeans. *"I'm afraid of heights."* Her voice sounded small and frightened to her own ears.

Jared stopped chewing for a moment and looked at her. He drank from his can of cola.

"What else?"

"What else?"

"What else are you afraid of? So far we have guns, enclosed spaces, and heights. And flying," he added as an afterthought.

"Does that make me hopeless?"

"Not completely hopeless. *Borderline, maybe.*"

Kendra looked up in time to see the amusement in his eyes and allowed herself to relax a bit. She picked up her sandwich again.

"I've been wondering about something," she said.

"Ask."

"Why did you start Double E? Where did you get the idea? Why is it successful?"

"I got the idea from the popularity of things like extreme skiing, where athletes look for a greater challenge. And I used to lead Outward Bound groups, before I joined Special Forces. Then there's my friend Michael Braden. He runs a camp for troubled youth—"

"Camp Sunrise?"

Jared looked up with interest. "You know about it."

"I know it well. My parents had completely given up on me and I was sent to Mike's program. I came very close to being his first failure. But he challenged me enough that I went back and finished high school.

"After I graduated I went on an Outward Bound trek," Kendra continued. "I think that's why I decided to join the army. I needed a challenge. *A physical challenge.* There wasn't anything we could do with me mentally."

"Double E works on both. Maybe that's why it's successful. We got a break when businesses picked up on it and began sending their executives."

"Why would businesses do that?"

"It all started with an ex-Special Forces commander who started his own company after he retired from the army. We knew each other and one day he called me up to lament that none of his sales people or directors had ever faced a real physical challenge.

"He knew from experience the confidence that is gained from facing something head on and succeeding. We talked for a while and I told him I would be getting back with him. Phil and Mark and I drew up a curriculum and faxed it to him. The next day I got a fax back asking for costs, schedules, and a list of a dozen names for my first class."

"And the rest is history," Kendra said.

"Well, close enough, anyway."

Kendra looked at him, eyes narrowed thoughtfully. "I don't hear a lot of enthusiasm. How long have you been doing this?"

"About seven years."

"And you're bored already?"

"I've been bored for at least six years."

"I see," Kendra said, her expression thoughtful.

He gaze swung to her. "What do you see?"

"What is there to challenge the best of the best? Of course you would be bored."

"It isn't that, really. I'm just tired of being the ultimate glorified baby sitter. One bad accident, one fatality, and I'm out of business." He sighed. "And the stupidity of the human race never fails to astound me. I often wonder if it has earned the right to survive."

Kendra laughed. "I've often thought the same." She studied him for a moment, wondering if she dared go where her thoughts led. She decided she had to. "Jared?"

He looked up, a brow quirked in question.

"Why me?"

He didn't ask what she meant. A corner of his mouth twitched and a dimple flashed in his cheek.

"You're a challenge, warrior woman. *For the best of the best.*" His dark gaze swept over her, searing in its intensity. "A challenge I can't resist. I don't know what the rules are, and I don't know what constitutes success, but I figure we'll find out together."

Kendra swallowed, nodded. "I'd like that."

Jared got to his feet and picked up the tray. "I'm going to turn in. Don't stay up too late. We'll be on the trail by sun-up."

Kendra looked around the room in dismay. Lighted only by the fire, shadows lurked in every corner. "And where do I sleep?"

"Where ever you'd like to unroll your sleeping bag."

"Here by the fire?" she asked hopefully.

"Why not? There's room for both of us." He went over to the door and dragged the bedrolls into the circle of light.

Kendra reached for hers and began unsnapping the fasteners and zipping the sides together.

Jared forced his body to relax, willed sleep to come. Tried to ignore the woman lying close enough to touch. Tomorrow night, if everything went as planned, they would be forced to share a sleeping bag. That would be all they shared, he vowed again, his teeth clenched.

Unwillingly, his mind replayed the scene at the waterfall, reliving again his fear when he saw Kendra lying at the bottom of the pool. His relief that she was all right and seemingly unconcerned about the fright she had given him caused him to snap and lose his hard won control.

He thought again of the single sleeping bag tomorrow night and debated whether or not to change the agenda. His intention to help Kendra overcome her multitude of fears and release the person frozen inside her without becoming emotionally entangled loomed ahead of him as a physical impossibility. He already wanted her far too much and he knew that a one night stand or even a hot steamy weekend with her would never be enough. Making love to Kendra would be a soul deep commitment for him, and until he had gained her trust, he could not take that risk.

Kendra sipped from her canteen and looked back down the valley at the terrain they had covered that morning.

"I wish I had my Bronco," she said without thinking.

Jared threw her a quizzical look. "Tired?"

"No." She recapped the flask and put it in her pack. "I would like to drive this valley. It's an off-roader's paradise."

Jared glanced over his shoulder, straightened in disbelief.

"You're kidding! No one can drive that course, in anything."

She grinned. "Wanna bet?"

He studied her. "Not a bet. How about a deal?"

"A deal?"

"Sure. You finish the program I've outlined for you, and I'll let you take my Jeep and drive to your heart's content."

"Will you come with me?"

"Sure. If you want me to."

"You have yourself a deal!" Kendra stuck out her hand.

Jared grasped her hand and she saw his smile disappear, felt his fingers tighten almost imperceptibly, then he turned away to shrug into his pack.

He did not look at her, but pointed to the wall of rock towering above them. "See that outcropping on the left, about two-thirds of the way up?"

Kendra swallowed. "I see it."

"That's our destination. It conceals the mouth of a cave where we will spend the night."

She tried to still her pounding heart, glanced around for a distraction. Found it. "Think we will get there before the storm?" she asked, proud of her seeming nonchalance.

Jared's glance at the sky told her he was already aware of the approaching weather system.

"I think that will depend on how honest you were about your climbing ability," he said, his eyes finally meeting hers, a challenge lurking in their depths.

Kendra straightened, her breath catching in indignation. "Well," she said, recovering her voice, "then we should get there snug and dry! Do you lead, or shall I?"

She had caught him by surprise, Kendra noted with satisfaction. Finally, a grin twisted his lips and he gestured for her to precede him.

"I wouldn't miss this for the world," he muttered under his breath.

Kendra heard and threw him one final glare before turning her attention to the cliff. The obstacle she had dreaded all day was now a challenge she couldn't resist.

CHAPTER EIGHT

Jared looked again at the clouds rolling toward them and reached out to steady Kendra as a gust threatened to peel her off the cliff. She had not exaggerated her climbing ability but the storm's approach was much faster than he had calculated.

"We have to find shelter!" he shouted above the noise of the wind.

She barely spared him a glance. "Yeah, right!"

"No. I'm serious. Angle to your left about a hundred yards. There's a chimney big enough to fit into."

"Both of us?" She reached for a handhold on an outcropping of rock.

"If we get real cozy," Jared replied.

"Not likely," she muttered under her breath, but the wind carried her words back to Jared. He grinned.

"Anything's possible. A little more to your left, about ten o'clock." The wind snatched the words away, but Kendra corrected her course.

The almost horizontal climb along the rock face with the wind tearing at them was even more wearing than the vertical ascent had been.

"Almost there," Jared yelled encouragement to Kendra. "Right where it looks like the wall ends. Keep going and you'll find yourself in the chimney."

He watched as she disappeared around a corner of rock and followed. He found her bent over, hands on her thighs, breathing hard. She straightened as he stepped in beside her.

"Some chimney," she said. "More like a closet and most welcome."

"Step over here and turn your back to the wind," Jared said as huge raindrops began pelting the rock around them. He jerked off his pack and untied a slicker to wrap around her.

"What about you?" Kendra asked, teeth chattering.

"I'll be okay."

"Sure you will." She handed him the raincoat. "You put it on and hold one side over me."

"Are you going to be difficult?" he grated.

"Of course. I've never had much time for martyrs. Besides, if you catch pneumonia and die, what happens to me?"

"I won't catch pneumonia. It's the middle of summer."

"You could fool me." Kendra shivered, still holding the garment out for him. "Okay." She let it fall. "If we go, we go together."

"You little fool!" Jared snatched at the slicker as the wind would have blown it away. He took one last look at her face before shrugging into it. "I hope you know what you're doing."

92

He reached out with one arm and pulled her against his chest, then pulled the coat closed around them both. He turned so that her back was against the rock face, completely sheltering her with his body.

"You're as safe as I can make you," Jared said as rain began to beat almost horizontally against the mountain side.

Kendra reached up to pull the hood more closely around his face. "Thank you," she whispered.

"Are you afraid of storms, too?" Jared asked, trying to distract himself from the feel of her pressed against his chest.

Kendra laughed, a deep husky sound. "No. Actually, I enjoy a good thunder storm. When I was a kid I would go out on the balcony and watch the lightning and wait for the thunder until the rain came. My parents never quite knew what to make of me."

"But you were afraid of the storm when we were in the plane," he reminded with a frown.

"I was afraid of being in a situation where I had no control," she explained.

"And this is different?" he asked, struggling to follow the intricacies of her thinking.

"Very different." She laid her head against his chest.

Jared stifled a groan, then winced as he felt hail begin to hit against his exposed back.

"What—?" Kendra stirred as the sound of hail against the rock face became almost deafening. "Jared, you—"

"Stay still!" he grated.

"But the hail! You're getting hit."

"Better me than you." His arms tightened until she stopped struggling. This time he focused on her softness and tried to ignore the stinging pain of the hail beating against him. His backpack would have offered some protection, he realized now, but it lay at his feet and there was no way he could get to it without exposing Kendra.

He felt her start to slip her arms around him and caught her hands.

"No, Kendra. You need to protect your hands from the hail. You could break a finger."

She caught her breath. "My God! *What is it doing to you?*"

He stopped her struggles in the most effective way he could think of, by covering her mouth with his.

"Jared." She drew in a sobbing breath.

"Relax, love," he whispered, his lips a fraction of an inch from hers, then he closed the distance again.

It was impossible to think, so Kendra gave herself up to the sensation of just feeling. Of being in Jared's arms, of having his lips against hers, tasting his warmth and sweetness. Feeling his hands as they molded her body to his.

Kendra groaned and raised her arms to put them around his neck. He let her and she realized the hail had stopped. The sun was coming out again and the last few raindrops were warm and gentle. She drew in a startled breath.

Jared apparently realized the storm was over at he same moment. He raised his head and let his arms drop from around her.

Kendra tried to step back and càme up against the rock face. She looked down to see several inches of hail covering the ground around them. Her eyes sought Jared's.

94

"Now what?" she asked.

He peeled off the slicker and reached down to pick up his backpack and shake the ice off it. He rolled up the slicker and tied it in place, then slipped the pack on and secured it. Finally he looked at Kendra again.

"We really need to wait until the sun dries the rock a bit. It's too dangerous to climb when it's wet like this."

"Do you think we will reach the cave before dark?" She looked over his shoulder to scan the sky. Her breath caught.

"What?" Jared glanced up and became still. Together they stared at the perfect rainbow below them.

"It almost makes the storm worth it," Kendra said, awe struck.

Jared grinned. *"Almost."* He shrugged and she saw him wince.

"You're hurt—" Kendra began, her eyes widening in concern.

"Of course not. What's a little hail to the *'best of the best'?"*

Kendra rolled her eyes. "Yeah. Right."

"Let's talk about why we're here," Jared said after a moment. "We've found a couple of things you aren't afraid of. What else?"

Kendra looked at him with open suspicion. "What do we have so far? *Besides storms?"*

"You don't appear to be afraid of water."

"No." Kendra felt her cheeks grow warm as she remembered the waterfall.

"What about animals? Cats? Dogs?"

"Dogs—definitely not. Cats? Small ones are all right. I haven't met your cougar yet." She looked at him from beneath her lashes.

"Do you still doubt that he's out here?" Jared looked at her, his expression stern.

Kendra shook her head.

"Does that knowledge frighten you?" Jared asked.

"No." She swallowed.

"If you were smart it would." He still frowned at her.

"I never claimed to be smart." She turned and began picking her way over the melting hail stones. "There's something else I'm not afraid of anymore."

"And what might that be?"

She looked back at him, held his gaze. *"You."*

Jared reeled as if he'd been struck. Shock rolled over him. He wasn't sure he wanted to know the answer, but he had to ask the question.

"Me? When were you ever afraid of me?" He tried to control his emotion, keep the harshness from his voice.

"From the moment I met you," Kendra almost whispered.

Jared raked a hand through his damp hair. Looked at her. "Are we talking real fear here?" This time the harshness was there.

"As real as it gets." Kendra did not meet his eyes.

"But why? What did I do—" He broke off with an abrupt intake of breath. "I see."

Her head jerked up. "What do you see?"

"It's the guns, isn't it? *It's still the guns!*"

"Jared, I said I'm not afraid of you anymore," Kendra repeated.

"But *why* were you afraid?"

She sighed. "Have you thought about the things I'm afraid of, and the things I'm not afraid of, and what they have in common?"

"Are you saying that when I make the connection, I'll understand why you are—were afraid of me?"

"Maybe." Her lips twitched. "I'll bet SueAnn would have already figured it out."

"Yeah, well, I don't claim to be nearly as good as SueAnn," Jared grinned. "But over the years, I've been able to put one of my degrees to good use."

"One of your degrees?" Kendra shook her head, her expression wistful. "I envy you and SueAnn. My high school diploma was a farce. I have a Masters in Strategic Intelligence from NDIC, but other than such specialized training, no real knowledge in any specific area."

Jared studied her. "And I say you put both SueAnn and me to shame. You've been through the hardest school in the world and you survived. And you did all that without becoming hard and callous."

She turned away, as if unable to face further scrutiny. "I wouldn't put me on too high a pedestal if I were you. I know from experience how hard it is to stay there."

Kendra stepped around the outcropping of rock and felt herself freeze. She swung around to face Jared.

"Cave? You did say cave. Why didn't that register? A small dark hole in the ground—probably with bats!" She shuddered. *"How could you?"* Her whole body trembled and she wrapped her arms around herself.

Jared pulled himself onto the ledge beside her.

"Kendra, you're overreacting," he said, his voice quiet and reasonable.

"I'm overreacting!" Her voice rose. "You know I'm claustrophobic, that I hate small dark places! I trusted you!" She glanced around wildly, looking for a place to run, found no where to go. Her gaze swung back to him. *"You planned this!"*

"Of course I planned this," Jared said. "What do you think we've been doing all day? We're working on overcoming your fears."

Her lips trembled and she licked them. "What—how is this supposed to help?"

The sun had disappeared behind the cliff and darkness fell around them. Jared glanced around.

"Kendra, we have to go inside. It will get cold very quickly now that the sun has set."

"How is spending the night in a cave going to help my claustrophobia?" she asked.

He sighed. "We're going to find out why you're afraid of small dark places. Once you can admit the reason, we're almost there."

"Oh, is that all?" Kendra asked. "Why didn't you say so? I could have told you down below."

He stared at her in the gathering darkness. "You mean you know?"

"I've always known." She shrugged. "But we're here and it's almost dark, so I guess there's no going back."

"Not tonight, I'm afraid." Jared pulled out a flashlight. "I'll show you around. It isn't really all that small, and it goes all the way through to an opening on the other side of the cliff."

98

Kendra forced herself to step inside and looked around as Jared flashed the light over the walls and ceiling of the cave.

"No bats," she said after a moment.

She saw his grin. "No bats. I promise. Notice the clean fresh smell. It's well ventilated. There's a smaller room back here. In fact, a few years ago, I dug a latrine, so we have almost all the comforts of home."

"Almost," Kendra said in relief. "If you don't mind, I'll borrow the flashlight and make use of those facilities."

"Be my guest."

Kendra found her way into a smaller adjoining section of the cave and immediately saw what she needed. A few minutes later, as she turned to leave, she froze, a small cry escaping her lips.

"Kendra?" Jared stood in the opening.

"What—what is it?" she asked, staring at two round orbs that caught the light and reflected it back at her.

She felt the jolt that shook him as he took the light from her hand. He played it around the corner of the room.

"It's an animal of some kind. Large."

"The cougar?" Kendra whispered.

"I don't think so—"

A feeble whine, pathetic and joyous at the same time, reached them.

"Jared, be careful!"

"It's a dog!" Jared knelt in the dirt. "And I know him. What are you doing here, old man?"

"How could he get up here?" Kendra wondered.

"It's a lot easier from the other side."

"So why bring me up the hard way?" she asked.

He didn't bother answering. The dog licked his hand and Jared reached to scratch behind his ear. The dog yelped in pain and snapped at him.

Jared jerked back. "He's hurt!" He played the light closer, drew in his breath. "He's tangled with something bigger and meaner than he is, with very sharp claws."

"The cougar."

"That's the first thing that comes to mind," he said dryly.

"What are we going to do?" she asked.

"About what?"

"The dog. Can we help him? At least give him water. He looks thirsty. If he drinks, it's a good sign."

Jared glanced at her. "You know a lot about dogs?"

"Enough."

"Okay. Bring a canteen."

"I have a cup I can fill." She turned away, froze.

"Take the flashlight," Jared said, holding it out to her.

Kendra hesitated, looked again at the darkness in front of her.

"No. I—you need it more than I do." She inched forward, holding her breath.

Her eyes adjusted and she felt her way toward the other room. Faint light from outside spilled in through the opening and she sighed in relief. She grabbed her canteen and a battered aluminum cup and started back toward the glow of light that surrounded Jared and the dog.

She knelt beside Jared and filled the cup. "Why don't I hold the light while you see if he will drink?" she suggested.

"Good idea." Murmuring soothing words, Jared held the cup so the dog could reach the water. After a few sniffs, he lapped cautiously, then greedily. Jared steadied the cup.

Kendra sighed in relief. "He's hurt, but maybe it isn't too bad."

"Why do you say that?"

"Animals are smarter than we are. If he had fatal injuries, he wouldn't drink. Why prolong the agony? He came in here to lick his wounds, not to die, like I thought he had."

"Should we try to feed him?" Jared asked.

"Let's wait until morning when we can get a better look. Any idea how long he's been here?"

Jared held his hand up to the light to examine the dark stain on it.

"The blood appears fresh, and the cut on his neck is still open. Probably only a few hours."

"Can you tell if he's bleeding heavily from any wound?"

Jared looked closer. "There's not much I can tell about blood on black fur in the dark."

Kendra dropped to her knees. "Let me try."

"Kendra," Jared said in alarm.

"I know what I'm doing. I've spent a lot of time working with dogs. You said you know him?"

"Yes. He belongs to a couple who live in the next valley. His name is Jack."

"As in *'the bean stalk*?"

"As in *'the box'*. Fast food. They found him outside the drive through of a *Jack-in-the-Box* restaurant late one night, bought him a *Jumbo Jack* and gained a friend for life."

Kendra straightened. "Well, I think they'll have him a bit longer. I can't find any deep bleeding cuts." She got to her feet. "How are we going to get this blood off our hands?"

Jared pulled a bandana from his pocket. "Try wetting this."

Kendra cleaned her hands as best she could and returned the damp cloth to him. She turned and made her way back into the larger room of the cave, oblivious now to the darkness.

CHAPTER NINE

Jared stood for a moment and looked at Kendra. She sat on the floor, knees drawn up and hands clasped around them. She had pulled out the jacket she wore earlier that morning and now huddled inside it.

"Are you all right?" Jared asked.

She looked up and he could see her smile in the dim light. "I'm fine."

"Aren't you supposed to be afraid or something? After all, this is still a small dark hole in the ground—or rather, a few thousand feet above ground."

"I've been thinking about that. I mean, what happened to the fear? I guess it's because the worst that can happen did happen."

"And what was that?" Jared had to ask.

"Well, I was afraid of bats. Instead I find a wounded animal that scares me half to death, but he turns out to be somebody's big friendly dog. I was afraid he might die, but now I think he'll be fine. So I don't know what's left to be afraid of. We've already pretty much run the gamut of my imagination."

Jared rubbed the back of his neck. "I have a couple of candles. I can light them if you'd like. Might keep the cougar away."

"Only if you think we need to. Actually, the darkness is rather soothing, and I can't see how small this place is."

"There should be a couple of cans of sterno around here somewhere. They'll work better and provide a little warmth, too." He walked over to a wall and worked a large flat rock loose. "Hey, I forgot about this." He turned and tossed a cotton throw to Kendra. "Wrap up in that while I get these going."

A couple of minutes later, two tiny fires flickered inside small flat cans.

"Shouldn't you put one in with Jack?" Kendra asked.

"I thought about that and remembered he has a fur coat. We don't."

"I was thinking the cougar could come in that entrance," Kendra said.

"Not likely. Besides, Jack would give us warning. And if I know Jack, our big cat is nursing a few wounds of his own."

Kendra grinned. "So he's a fighter, is he?"

"He's that." Jared looked at her. "The two of you have a lot in common. He isn't afraid of anything—or at least not the things you would think he had enough sense to be afraid of."

He saw her wince. "Something else we have in common," she said. "He has to learn the hard way."

Jared rummaged through his back pack and handed her a can of protein drink.

"Civilian MREs?" she asked with a grin. "I guess you can't get much more *ready-to-eat* than this."

"Here's a couple of protein food bars." He tossed one to her and noticed again that she caught it with one hand.

He found a seat facing her and opened his drink. "You have excellent hand to eye coordination," he said after a moment.

He felt Kendra's glance but could not interpret it in the near darkness.

She shrugged. "Thanks, I guess. It's just one of those things that happen."

"You were born with it?"

"Aren't most people?"

"I'm not sure. I know a lot of people have to work at it, and some never achieve it."

"I guess I've always taken it for granted."

Jared let a short silence reign as they finished their meal. He put the empty cans and wrappers in a plastic bag and put it beside his pack.

"Are we ready to talk about your fear of small dark places?" he asked. "You said you knew the origin."

She sighed and stretched out her legs. "If you thought about it, you could figure it out. Remember, I told you they put me in a straight jacket in a padded cell?"

Jared tensed. "How could your parents allow that?"

"Oh, they had no choice. I was very self-destructive." She pushed up her sleeves and held out her arms, let them fall. "Well, you can't see them now, but I have scars from scratching myself with my fingernails. I pulled out my hair by the handful. But the funny thing is I couldn't feel any pain."

She paused for a moment. "Anyway, back to the padded cell, *my small dark cave.* I had no control at all. I had no choice about eating. They put me on an IV. I had no choice about sleeping. They sedated me. They decided when to turn the lights on or off. I existed for what seemed an eternity, and every day I felt the little sanity I had left slipping away. I had no hope.

"If you think about the things that I'm not afraid of, such as storms, well, what's to worry about? I may not be in control, but if I get struck by lightning, it will be a quick and painless death. *Water?* Well, they say drowning is one of the least painful ways to die.

"You know why I avoid guns. Now you know about caves. What else? *Heights.* Again, I don't have as much control as I would like. The same with flying. It's all about control. I guess SueAnn would call me a control freak. She's probably right. It's just—ever since Bobby—I've tried to control everything—" She broke off, jammed her hands into her pockets.

"And what it is about me that you can't control?" Jared asked before he could consider the wisdom of the question.

"I beg your pardon?"

"You said when I understood the connection, I would know why you were afraid of me."

"Actually, I said maybe." He could see her smile in the darkness.

"Okay, so help me out."

"I don't think you need help. It will come to you soon enough." She yawned. "Dare I ask about sleeping arrangements?"

"We only have one sleeping bag," Jared said.

"I thought as much. You wouldn't let me carry anything. I'm glad you didn't try to carry two."

"Actually, there is another reason I only brought one. *Part of your cure.*" Jared watched her reaction.

"That sounds interesting. I may get into this program, yet." She got to her feet, stretched.

"However, I'm not sure you still need it."

"What?" She looked at him. "The cure or the sleeping bag?"

"You aren't taking this seriously, are you?"

She turned away, hugged her arms across her chest. "You must be doing something right. At least I'm not afraid of you."

"Because you can control me?" he asked.

"No. Because I know you have enough control for both of us." Her voice was a whisper of sound in the stillness.

A surge of emotion rocked Jared to the soles of his feet. He forced himself to remain where he stood.

He swallowed and willed his voice to sound normal. "Come here, Kendra."

She turned to look at him as if unsure she had heard right. He held out his arms.

Kendra wet her lips. "What—what are you doing?"

"I need to hold you."

"Is that a good idea?"

"I'll let you decide."

She closed her eyes. Swallowed. "Do you have any idea how much I've wanted you to hold me?"

"I hope as much as I want to hold you."

"I've always fought against feelings that were so consuming. I could never afford the distraction."

"Neither could I."

"So what's different now?" She opened her eyes and looked at him.

"Now I'm in control and you're going to help me stay that way. I'm going to hold you until you relax, then we'll crawl into the sleeping bag and go to sleep. Tomorrow, we'll worry about Jack and the cougar, and whatever else is out there. We'll face it together."

"Together," she whispered. She took a step toward him. Another.

With a groan Jared reached for her. He wrapped his arms around her and buried his face against her neck. Soft curves fused with hard planes and a single shadow danced against the wall of the cave.

Kendra lay for a moment, suspended in the momentary unreality between sleep and wakefulness. She basked in the warmth of the sleeping bag, felt the security of Jared's arms around her. Her eyes opened and she could see the opening to the cave, lighter now as day began to break. Time to get up. An unconscious groan escaped.

Jared awoke in a heartbeat. "What's wrong?" His arms tightened.

Kendra groaned again, deliberately this time. "Don't do that."

"What am I doing?"

"I'm trying to convince myself to get up. You aren't helping."

"What's the rush?" he asked.

"You know the answer to that as well as I do." She began unzipping the sleeping bag.

Jared propped himself on one elbow. "In my fantasies about you, I've wondered if your voice would be even huskier first thing in the morning. Now I know. It is."

Kendra gave an exaggerated sigh. "Geez, and here I've been thinking you might have something else in mind. Now that I know it's only my voice, I can relax." She crawled from between the covers and stood up.

"I wouldn't be too sure of that," Jared drawled. "You happen to have just about the sexiest voice I've ever heard."

"That line won't get you anywhere, Major!"

"I didn't think it would. I'm merely giving you fair warning." He sat up and Kendra turned away, trying to put distance between them. He looked too sexy on all counts. For now he didn't want her in his bed, didn't want to want her. Okay, she would play along, make it easy for him. Her time would come.

Kendra picked up her canteen and backpack and went through to the other room. She splashed water on her face and arms and gave her teeth a quick brushing. Jack raised his head weakly and she bent over to see that his eyes were clear and alert. She drew a breath of relief. He did not seem to be experiencing any symptoms of shock.

She stroked his head gently. "We'll fix you up as soon as we can see what we're doing," she promised. "You're a nice tough dog and you'll be just fine."

Kendra straightened and stepped back into the larger room of the cave. Sunlight now poured through the opening and she could see that Jared had stripped off his shirt and stood with a towel around his neck.

Kendra gasped and rushed toward him. "Jared! *Your back!*"

He turned and caught her wrist as she put out a hand to touch the bruises and welts that covered his back and shoulders. She stopped abruptly and swallowed, but made no attempt to mask what she knew he could see in her eyes.

"You're hurt!" she whispered, blinking away tears. "When you protected me from the hail, that's what happened to you!"

"And I would do it again in a heart beat."

Kendra brought her other hand to her mouth, her fingers trembling. "And how do you think that makes me feel, to see you hurt and know it's my fault?"

Their gazes locked for what seemed an eternity. At last Jared released her and turned away.

"Is there anything—?" Kendra began.

"No." He grabbed his shirt and disappeared into the other room.

Her hands still shaking, Kendra sat down on the bedroll to pull on her boots. "Get a grip!" she told herself impatiently. "You've seen worse injuries. He'll live!"

Jared decided they would carry Jack down the mountain and take him home. He gave the dog an injection of antibiotics, pain killer and a sedative. While waiting for the last two to kick in, he tossed Kendra a food bar.

"We can have real food for lunch," he explained. "We'll have Jack home by then."

Kendra nodded. "Since you'll be carrying Jack, I'll carry the backpacks."

Jared started to protest, saw the determination on her face, and shrugged. "That's fair enough, I guess."

"Actually, it isn't, but I know you won't let me carry the bedroll, too."

He grinned. "You learn fast."

Kendra held his gaze. "Not fast enough, it seems." She turned away.

Jared watched as she slipped into her backpack and looped his over her shoulder. After a moment he picked up the bedroll and strapped it across his shoulders, then bent to lift the big dog, now a dead weight in his arms.

"Let's hope our friend, the cougar, doesn't choose this time to pay a visit," Jared said dryly.

Kendra threw him a look that said she was thinking the same thing.

"I'll go first," Jared said. "I know the trail better than you and—" Seeing her expression he broke off. "Well, let's just leave it at I'll go first."

Kendra laughed and sketched a snappy salute. "Aye, aye, Major Macho. I've got your back." *At least she would enjoy the view*, she added to herself.

Kendra didn't see it coming, had no time to prepare. One moment she was engrossed in watching the muscles in Jared's back, arms, and legs as he struggled down the slope with his arms full of limp dog. The next she almost bumped into him as he came to an abrupt halt on the trail.

"Don't move!" he whispered fiercely.

The blood curdling cry of a cougar rent the air from mere feet away. Peering around Jared, she could see it blocking the trail ahead, perhaps ten yards further along.

She had no time to think, merely acted on instinct. She crouched, sliding Jared's backpack off her shoulder. His gun appeared in her hand as if by magic. She slid the safety off and raised it to take aim.

It had been a long time since Jared had been caught so totally off guard. Not only did he have his arms full, he couldn't have gotten to his backpack even if he had been able to drop Jack. His options, or lack thereof, flashed through his mind in rapid succession as the cougar snarled again and began to move forward. In a few steps it had reached the running stride that preceded a leap. Maybe he could step aside at the last minute, Jared thought desperately. Where was Kendra—

The gun going off a few feet to his left spun Jared around in time to see Kendra fire a second shot. She lowered the gun, looking intently ahead.

Jared remembered the cougar and jerked around. The animal stretched full length a few feet away, unmoving. Jared placed Jack on the ground and walked over to touch the animal with his foot, then bent for a closer look.

Jared looked at Kendra. "One shot through the jugular. The other— the other broke his neck! How—what—"

Kendra shrugged, checked that the safety was on, and let the gun slip from her hand. It fell to clatter against a rock. She stood slowly.

"I never could miss with one of those things." She gave a half hearted smile and closed her eyes. As Jared started toward her, she collapsed at his feet.

"What happened here?" Phil and a paramedic named Jim rushed into the clearing where Jared sat against a tree, Kendra's head cradled in his lap. Jack lay by his side and Jared idly stroked the sedated dog with his left hand, his right tangled in Kendra's hair.

"*Geez!*" Jim exclaimed as he spotted the dead cougar. After a stunned moment, he knelt beside Jared. "What seems to be wrong with her?"

"In a nutshell," Jared said, "she has been morbidly afraid of handguns for twelve years—since her little brother was killed with one. When the cougar appeared on the trail, she reached in my backpack, pulled out my .45, shot the cougar once through the jugular and once through the neck, said something

112

about not ever being able to miss with one of those things, and fainted at my feet." He glanced at his watch. "That was almost three hours ago. She still hasn't come around."

Jim was examining Kendra, checking her pulse and looking into her eyes with a pen light. "Sounds a lot like a variation on post-traumatic stress syndrome, but whether it's been suppressed for twelve years or came about as a result of shooting the cougar—that had to be pretty frightening in itself— someone else will have to make that call. Mark is setting down about a quarter of a mile from here and a couple of the guys will be here with a stretcher. Her vitals all look good. When we get her on board, I'll set up an IV, but there isn't much we can do right now."

Phil knelt beside Jared and handed him a bottle of water. "SueAnn will meet us in Denver. Meanwhile, she's trying to reach Kendra's family. She was able to get a name and address from her military records, but hadn't been able to reach anyone when we left."

Jared drank the water automatically and handed the bottle back to Phil.

"I'm not sure that's a good idea," he said, his voice sounding ragged.

"What isn't?"

"Contacting Kendra's family. I got the feeling she isn't close to them."

Phil shrugged. "She listed them as emergency contacts. What else can we do?"

"Nothing." He looked down at Kendra's face for a moment, now relaxed and vulnerable. "Maybe it's for the best. Maybe her exile in Hell is about to end."

CHAPTER TEN

Kendra became aware of voices. Subdued, muted voices. Who were they discussing? And why didn't they want her to hear? She tried to sit up, found she could not move. *Struggled to free her arms.* Panic washed over her. She tried to scream.

And made no sound.

Jared glanced toward the bed in time to see Kendra try to sit up. He saw the terror when she realized her arms had been strapped to the bed. Saw her mouth open, braced him self for the scream. *And heard no sound.*

Jared froze for a moment and then raced toward the bed.

"Get these restraints off now!" he ordered as he began struggling with the fasteners.

"You can't do that, sir!" the nurse protested. "We have to have—"

Jared swung toward Beverly Allen.

"Mrs. Allen," he grated, "I don't know if you have any idea what being in a straight jacket did to Kendra twelve years ago, but trust me, you can't let her go through that again."

She put a trembling hand to her mouth, her eyes desperate as she sought her husband.

"Do as he says, young lady," Jim Allen told the nurse. "I will take full responsibility."

"Thank you, sir." Jared had the straps off now and he caught Kendra's right hand in his, gently chafing it. "You're free now, Kendra. There's nothing to be afraid of. Open your eyes again. It's Jared."

He saw her lashes flutter, saw her try to wet her lips.

"Jared?"

He bent to hear her better.

"Yes, love?"

She licked dry lips. "The—cougar?"

"He's dead. There's nothing to be afraid of now."

"Jack?"

Jared felt his lips twitch. "Jack is fine. Being spoiled rotten by the paramedics, but doing great."

"And you?"

Jared struggled to speak, squeezed her hand.

"Jared?" She sounded worried. "Are you all right?"

He swallowed, couldn't keep the huskiness from his voice.

"I am now," he said. He bent to press his lips to her forehead.

Her eyes opened. "That's—one lousy kiss. I know you can do better—"

Jared couldn't stop his grin. "No doubt. But there's someone else here who would like a word with you." He reached for Beverly's hand and placed Kendra's in it.

"Mom?"

Jared heard everything in that one word. *Love. Fear. Hope. Betrayal.*

"What happened? Why are you here?"

Jared pulled the door closed behind him.

"Young man. *Major Hall.*" Jared turned reluctantly to see Jim Allen hurrying toward him as he waited for the elevator. He jammed his hands in his pockets and braced himself.

Jim Allen reached him and took a moment to catch his breath. "Do you have a moment? Could we get a cup of coffee or something?"

Jared stared at him.

Jim shrugged, a self-conscious shrug. "I want to ask you about my daughter. I've—never met any of her friends."

Jared looked down. "I'm not all that sure I'm her friend."

"Oh, I'd say you're a lot more than that," Jim said dryly. "At least she thinks you are."

"Friends don't put friends in a position to get themselves killed to prove a point," Jared said. "If your daughter was not the strongest, bravest—" He broke off and swallowed as his voice wavered on the edge of breaking.

When he had himself under control again, he went on. "If it weren't for her courage and marksmanship, there would be three bodies on that trail now—mine, hers, and the dog we were caring for. And that would be my fault."

"And why is that?" Jim asked. His kind blue eyes swept over Jared before returning to meet his gaze. "I can't find anything to fault in your appearance, but as fine a specimen of manhood as you are, you're not God. You can't accept responsibility for things you can't control. You can only thank Him for his intervention."

Jared began to tremble, felt him self losing control. Jim's arm slipped around his shoulder.

"Let's see about that coffee," Jim said, turning him away from the elevators. Zombie like, Jared allowed himself to be guided down a hallway and into a secluded coffee shop. He almost fell into the booth and propped his arms on the edge of the table to keep himself upright.

Jim shoved a mug of coffee in front of him and pushed a basket containing sugar packets and creamer within his reach.

"May I ask how long since you've slept?" Jim asked.

Jared glanced at his watch and realized that the hands and digits there meant nothing to him. He placed his other hand over it, shook his head.

"I don't—" His voice sounded rusty and cracked, so he sipped his coffee, black and bitter, and tried again. "I don't even know what day it is, or whether it's day or night."

"I thought as much." Jim studied him as he added cream to his own coffee. "Tell me again how you aren't Kendra's friend."

Jared sighed, noticed a fine tremor in his hand as he reached for his coffee. He drew his hand back.

"Do you know what I do for a living, sir? The training programs—"

"I talked with your friend, Phil, and the helicopter pilot. I think I have a pretty good picture."

"Well, Kendra's expedition had to be aborted, at least her participation in it. But before that happened, I got to know her well enough to realize she has some serious issues she needs to deal with. I had already told her that we could tailor individual programs and offered to design one for her. She was hesitant at first. Maybe I pushed her too hard—"

"Maybe she needed to be pushed," Jim suggested.

"She almost lost her life." Jared's voice was flat and very controlled.

"But instead, she saved not only her own life, but yours, as well. No one knows about her fear of guns as well as I do, or how deep it goes. She was training to try out for the Olympic pentathlon when her brother was killed. Her edge was her marksmanship with a pistol. Apparently she hasn't lost any of that skill. And she was where she was for one reason and one reason only. That is where the good Lord wanted her to be. You can't take credit for that."

Jared continued to stare at this gentle man who in his own way was as intriguing as his daughter. Before he could come up with a reply, a waitress appeared with a bowl of soup and a plate of crackers and cheese.

"I didn't figure you had bothered to eat, either," Jim said dryly.

As the aroma of the soup reached his nostrils, Jared felt his stomach respond. "I'm not sure," he said. "I think Phil drug me off somewhere and fed me, but I don't know how long ago that was."

"Please, eat up," Jim invited.

Jared pulled the bowl toward him and reached for a handful of crackers. "Why are you doing this, sir?" He asked before scooping up a spoonful of soup and bringing it to his mouth.

"Because I recognize the symptoms. I couldn't help my daughter twelve years ago, but maybe I can help you."

Jared swallowed. "Symptoms?"

"*Guilt.* Just as Kendra insists on shouldering the blame for her brother's death, you are trying to assume responsibility for what *could* have happened to her."

"I was responsible for her safety. She trusted me. I told her that unless she trusted me completely, there was no point in going through with the training. And then I—"

Jim was shaking his head. "I've heard almost the identical words from Kendra. She was the babysitter. She was in charge. She was supposed to be taking care of the boys."

Jared finished the soup. As he reached for his coffee again, he noticed that his hand was almost steady. He looked up to meet Jim's eyes.

"So why are we here?" Jared asked.

"What are your plans now?" Jim asked in lieu of an answer.

Jared shrugged. "Mark and Phil have hung around to fly me back to my cabin. I'll lick my wounds for a few days and then rejoin the program."

"Just like that?"

Jared quirked a brow, letting his silence ask the question for him.

"No good-by for Kendra? No farewell kiss. No—"

"I think you know I can't do that, sir. You've pointed out that I'm not God. Neither am I Superman. I'm no good for your daughter. She—"

"She deserves a chance to decide that."

Jared was thoughtful for a moment before shaking his head. "Sorry, sir. Thanks for the coffee and the concern. I wish I could be the man you think I am—"

"You only have to be the man Kendra thinks you are," Jim said, his gaze holding Jared's.

'…I don't believe it's open season on mercenaries. And do we really want one?'

Jared allowed himself to remember Kendra's words to SueAnn and a cynical smile twisted his lips. "Oh, I understand very well the kind of man she thinks I am." He pushed back his chair and held his hand out to Jim. "I wish you luck, sir. Take care of her. I know your family has been through a lot. I hope you have your daughter back."

Jim stood to take the outstretched hand. "If I do, it's all thanks to you, Major Hall. You are the first person who has been able to get through to her in twelve years."

'You might not have realized I was a woman when you rescued us in Kuwait, but I knew you were a man, the only one to ever touch my soul.'

Jared shook off the sound of Kendra's words, tried to forget her husky voice. Unable to speak, he released Jim's hand and turned away, walking with quick strides out of the coffee shop and back toward the elevators.

Maybe Kendra's exile in Hell was over. But his was just beginning. He had only himself to blame. He had known better.

Lose…lose…lose…

Kendra stared at her father. The color drained from her face and she wet her lips. "He's gone! But I—" She sank back against the pillows. "I guess that means I failed the program. *That there is no hope for me!*"

Jim sat down on the bed beside her and took her hands in his. He could feel the fine tremor in them and his hold tightened.

"Do *you* think you failed? It sounds to me like you passed with flying colors. No one could have done a better job under the circumstances. And I think *your* Major needs to know that in no uncertain terms."

Kendra watched him, her expression openly suspicious. She wet her lips again, and a glimmer of hope shone through the hurt in her eyes.

"Yeah?"

"*Yeah.* You are going to move forward from today as if you had won Olympic gold. And when you are strong again, you can face him on his own terms, and he will have to back down. He's gone because he thinks he failed you by putting you in danger. But when you were tested, you came through. He has to know that, but you are the only one who can show him."

Jim watched the light of battle replace the despair in his daughter's eyes. Although she had chosen to estrange herself from her family for years, he still knew her. Knew her as well as he knew his own mind. She had always been *Daddy's girl* and reacted to things in the same way he did. Major Hall wouldn't know what hit him.

"He'll go back to his cabin for a few days. Make sure Jack is all right. Climb the mountain again. I want to drive the Bronco out there. That way, if worse comes to worse, I can lick my wounds by four-wheeling through that valley. I tell you, Dad, that place is an off-roader's paradise. I—"

"Whoa! Slow down, sweetheart. You can't go yet. They still want to run some tests—and your boss is on his way to see you."

Her eyes widened. "My boss?"

"I know it's all confidential, but apparently he has some more information about why you couldn't complete the original expedition with

Major Hall's group. And a few questions for you."

"When will he get here?"

"Tomorrow before noon."

"Will I have all the tests done by then so I can leave as soon as he is through with me?"

Jim reached out to squeeze her hand. "I'll see what I can do to expedite things."

The next morning a conservatively dressed Kendra sat with a three star general in the relative privacy of the coffee shop. She apologized for not having access to her uniform, and he shook his head dismissively before taking a sip of coffee.

"That's part of what we need to discuss, Agent Allen. Do you think the uniform still fits? Are you comfortable with it?"

She understood what he was asking and paused to consider her answer. "The uniform still fits, sir. It's when I'm not in it that I begin to lose my edge."

"I've been thinking the same thing. We've sent you under too many times. Your cover is bound to be compromised, and I think that happened on this last mission. We're still doing damage control on that. In fact, Major Hall and his group are looking into it, as well."

Kendra drew a careful breath. "What does that mean, sir?"

"Apparently some sort of tracking device was planted on you, or in something that you always had with you. It's not *in* you. That was covered in one of the series of tests you underwent yesterday. They were suspicious long before you decided to abort the mission, and they wanted to make sure they could find you if you disappeared."

"But how—what—?" Kendra sputtered.

"We were hoping you could help with that. We're thinking that it had to be something—maybe a piece of jewelry—that you never took off, unless maybe it would get wet. Does anything come to mind?"

Kendra shook her head. "But how did they manage to plant something inside—on—whatever we're looking for? I mean, they—" She broke off.

"You thought of something."

"Possibly." She closed her eyes for a moment. "There was one evening, a couple of days before I left. I poured a cup of coffee and went to my desk. The next thing I knew, I woke up. I had fallen asleep. I was disoriented. My hair had come loose from the clasp—" She paused.

"What kind of clasp? Do you have it with you?"

"No. I left everything at Major Hall's cabin. We were going to climb a mountain that day and I didn't want to take a chance on losing anything. Whatever I might have worn, a locket, a bracelet, I left behind that day. We were gone overnight and I never got back to the cabin."

"Back to when you fell asleep. Did anything seem out of place, other than your hair being loose?"

"Nothing registered. I was pretty groggy and thought I must be exhausted. I would have blamed myself for anything out of the ordinary."

"Did anything fit that description?"

"Not that I recall. There was something that bothered me at the time, but I can't remember what it was, exactly."

"This could be critical."

"I understand that." She studied him. "Why is this still important, sir? Do you think someone else will be coming after me?"

She had only been half serious as she asked the question and was totally unprepared for the general's reply.

"We can't rule out that possibility, Agent."

She drew a careful breath. "That means Major Hall could be in danger—if whatever was bugged is still at his cabin."

"We've alerted his team to that possibility."

"Have you alerted him?"

"We haven't been able to reach him." General Starr glanced at his watch. "I will need an answer from you in a couple of weeks on whether or not you plan to stay with us, Agent. Is that satisfactory?"

"Yes, sir. I will have made a decision by then."

CHAPTER ELEVEN

Jared stood on an outcropping of rock and swept the valley with his binoculars, remembering the last time he had performed a similar act. The same sense of foreboding had been hovering just out of focus for a couple of days. He couldn't pinpoint the cause of his unease. More like a feeling of impending doom. He felt a sudden urge to get in touch with his team, but he had left his radio behind. He would have to wait until he got back to the cabin, still several hours away, considering he was almost halfway up the mountain.

Clouds loomed ominously and he paused for a moment to remember the storm he and Kendra had weathered on this same mountain. What could he have been thinking, to put her in such danger? He hadn't just lost his edge, as she had been quick to point out. He seemed to have lost it completely.

He shifted the weight of his backpack to a more comfortable angle, noting with satisfaction that the bruises from the hail a week ago no longer caused him pain. The bruises to his soul—well, those were better left for future analysis.

A persistent thrumming sound kept gnawing at the edge of his consciousness, and Jared paused to raise his binoculars again. A helicopter, at first a mere speck on the horizon, grew larger and larger, circled the valley and finally set down a couple of miles from his cabin. Jared recognized it as one that belonged to his company. But why was it *here*? And in this weather? He hastened his descent and set a course to intercept his visitors.

"It's about time you showed up." Phil's disgruntled voice followed his hand as it shot out from a clump of bushes to pull Jared off the trail. "We've been trying to reach you for days."

Jared allowed himself a few seconds to recoup from the shot of adrenaline that had him ready to take someone apart.

"You should know better than to pull something like that," he said, rubbing the side of his neck.

"Well, it was the best I could come up with. We're being watched."

Jared looked at him. "Talk to me."

"The only thing we're certain of is that Kendra was bugged before she left Germany."

Jared felt another jolt of adrenaline to his system. *"Was? Or is?"*

"We don't think she is now, but since we don't know where they hid the bug, we can't be sure. She told her boss that she left everything here."

"So all we have to do is find the device—is she still being followed?"

"We can't rule out that possibility. That's a quote from the three star general who is her boss."

"So where is she now?" Jared looked from Phil to Mark who stood slightly to one side.

Neither man spoke. Phil looked out over the valley and Mark became very interested in his boots.

"I asked, *where is Kendra now?*" Jared ground out the words.

Mark cleared his throat. "We came here hoping you could tell us."

"I left her in Denver with her parents."

"They took her home several days ago."

"Home?"

"To Seattle."

Jared waited.

"As soon as she could pack, she jumped in her Bronco and started driving east. She has not checked in with her parents since she left, but they did not expect her to. They are sure she was coming here."

Jared didn't ask why Kendra would come here. That she might had been at once his fondest hope and his worst nightmare. A shiver of apprehension snaked down his spine.

"I've been on the mountain for a couple of days," he explained.

"Without a radio?"

Jared shrugged. "It seemed like a good idea at the time." He met Phil's gaze. "Didn't we leave this all behind?"

"When it involves our nation's security and someone we love, how can we leave it behind? It seems to find us."

Jared studied the faces of these men who were so much more than friends. "So do we have any kind of plan?"

127

"When we circled the valley, we saw a *camo* jeep down in a ravine. It wasn't here when we picked up Kendra."

"So we can count on their being at the cabin?"

"At least within sight of it."

"And they will know you are here?"

"They will know the helo landed. If they haven't seen you before this, maybe they will think we just dropped you off. We left a team with it. Mark is going to go back and fly it over the ridge where he will wait for a call. The rest of us will stay out of sight while you saunter up to the cabin as if you had just returned."

Jared drew a hand over his mouth. "Someone is out there. I've felt it for several hours. I couldn't see anything." He touched the binoculars around his neck, looked back at Phil. "So who is following her? Not the same guys?"

"Not the same ones, but part of the same group. They were apparently able to get a message out for someone else to pick up the trail."

"So what did she uncover, or is that so classified—"

"It's way beyond my security clearance. I don't know about yours. This lady is one of the most effective agents in the DIA."

"Why doesn't that surprise me?" Jared grumbled.

"Well, a match made in Heaven, as they say."

"Meaning what?" Jared shot Phil a glance.

"That as good as she is at getting into trouble, you're—or rather we're—better at getting her out of it."

Jared didn't bother to answer. He slipped back into his pack. "No point in putting this off. Do you need some time, or do I head for the cabin?"

Kendra raised her binoculars and slowly swept the valley below. She had pulled over when she saw the helicopter circling the valley. She had watched it land, seen two men leave and only one return. Several then disembarked and the craft lifted off to tuck in behind a ridge in the next valley. She was pretty sure that it was one of the Double E helicopters.

She paused in her sweep and slowly returned. There! Some kind of jeep in a camo paint job. *Now why would anyone want to hide something like that?* She reached for her cell phone.

Jared tried to think around the pain splitting his skull. He slit an eyelid with deliberate precision and bright light stabbed straight through to his brain. *What had they used to bash in his head?*

He slowly and unobtrusively did body inventory. He did not appear to be bound or gagged. And that meant? Either they thought he was already dead—and he wasn't sure they were that far off target—or they wanted to make it easy for him to try and escape. Why? So they could shoot him in the attempt. He reminded himself of the two expedition members who had been executed and impersonated.

"...you've been out of the military for several years. Maybe you've lost your edge." Kendra's contemptuous summation rang in his ears. How right she was! He'd proven her point by letting them get cornered by the cougar. And now this? He'd walked straight into their trap, knowingly, and been neutralized before he could lift a finger.

As these thoughts raged through his mind, he subconsciously listened for any sounds that his captors were still in the cabin. He'd figured out by now that he'd been dragged into the storeroom. The door was probably barred. *Not that that would be a problem.* Taking a chance that he was alone, he raised himself to his hands and knees. Waiting for the dizziness to pass, he managed to reach a kneeling position. Just as he started to stand, an explosion flung him back against the wall and he could hear the roar of flames.

So, he thought grimly, they weren't going to bother executing him during an escape attempt. They intended to burn him alive. *Who were these people and what had Kendra done to them?*

The blast from the explosion rocked Kendra. She swung her binoculars toward the cabin to see it totally engulfed in flames. Where was Jared? She didn't even know if he was here. As she continued to search desperately for signs of life, she saw two figures break away from the cabin and head in the direction of the concealed jeep. Just as she was about to drop the binoculars and follow them, she saw a flicker of movement from the corner of her eye and swung back. A prone figure drug itself from beneath the house, which appeared to be on the verge of collapse. She dropped back into the driver's seat, shoved a CD into the stereo and threw her Bronco into gear.

Jared struggled for breath, the heat from his burning cabin scorching his skin. He had to get further away, but he had used all his strength escaping through the trapdoor in the store room and crawling from beneath the house.

"I'm standing my ground in this lonesome town... No one else around..."

Jared thought he had finally lost it completely, imagining he heard music. He struggled to lift his head and saw a dark red Bronco barreling across the valley toward him. With a supreme effort he pulled himself to his feet.

The vehicle skidded to a stop a few feet from him and the passenger door opened. "Get in!" Kendra said. She gunned the engine.

Jared would never know how he found the strength to take those few steps that brought him to the side of the Bronco. He fell into the seat and Kendra reached over to pull him the rest of the way inside and close the door.

And then he wondered whether he might have been safer had he taken his chances with his unknown assailants. Kendra headed straight down into the valley. He looked up to see that she had set a course to intercept a couple of fleeing figures. And she wasn't bothering to go around any obstacles.

He tried to speak and his voice came out cracked and high-pitched. *"Are you insane?"*

She threw him a cocky grin. "Certifiably, Major. And it's good to see you, too." She downshifted to take a hill and they momentarily lost sight of her quarry. "But I intend to end this now!" As they crested the hill, the two running figures were just in front of them.

"What are you planning to do?"

"Whatever it takes to detain them for Phil and his men." She reached for something under the seat. "Take the wheel for a moment."

Miraculously, Jared's head cleared as he grabbed for the steering wheel she had abandoned.

"Just keep going straight." She pulled herself up until she was standing in the seat with her upper body sticking through the sun roof.

"You can't—" Jared forgot whatever admonition he had been about to issue as he saw first one and then the other of the two men seemingly trip over their own feet and fall headlong.

"I've got it!" Kendra dropped into the driver's seat and slammed on the brakes to skid to a stop mere inches from the first prone body. She threw open the door and sprang from the vehicle, snatched up a rifle that had been dropped, and aimed it with deadly intent at the man who was beginning to stir.

"Kendra, look out—"

She whirled, the gun she held discharging to send the rifle flying from the hands of the other assailant.

In the confusion that followed, she heard the sound of the helicopter overhead just as Phil arrived with a group of men. The rotors threw up dirt and rocks as the craft set down a few yards away.

When Phil and his team had the prisoners secure, Kendra turned back to see Jim working over Jared who had slumped over in the seat. Phil rushed to help while Mark and another paramedic brought a stretcher from the helicopter.

Kendra dropped the rifle and rushed to the Bronco. "What happened?" she asked.

"Take it easy," Phil said. "He has a nasty bump on the head, probably a concussion, and he inhaled a lot of smoke. We have to get him to a hospital."

Kendra put a trembling hand to her mouth. Mark slipped an arm around her. "Do you want to come with us in the helicopter?" he asked. "I can have one of the guys drive your car—"

"I can't," Kendra said, not taking her eyes off Jared. "I have to check out a couple of things. Where are you taking him?"

"The same place we took you."

"I'll get there as soon as I can."

"Let me stay and drive back with you," Phil offered as he joined them.

Kendra shook her head. "Take care of Jared. I won't be long."

Phil's gaze sought and held hers. "You know, you just did a great job. Probably saved several lives. These guys play for keeps."

Kendra nodded a curt thanks. "That's why I have to finish this now. And it won't be over until I find whatever they tagged me with."

132

Phil looked at the cabin. "Nothing could have survived that inferno."

"Maybe what we're looking for never got into the cabin."

"I can't leave you here alone," Phil said. "It's not the way we do things. Besides, Jared would kill me."

Kendra turned to watch Jared being loaded aboard the helicopter. She looked at Phil and shook her head. "Major Hall doesn't want to have anything more to do with me. Can you blame him? Just knowing me almost got him killed today, and look at his cabin. He's lost everything because of me."

"The cabin was never that important to him. On the other hand, you are. You have to know that, Kendra—"

"Sure," she drawled, marveling that she was able to keep the tears from her voice. "That's why he couldn't get away from the hospital fast enough." She looked up at the man beside her. "Don't worry, Phil. I'm a big girl now. I can take care of myself. And now that I've thought about it, I won't be driving to Denver. There's no point. Besides, I have a mission to complete."

She picked up the night sticks she had used to stop the suspects and walked over to the Bronco. She turned back to give Phil a snappy salute, then stepped into the vehicle. Throwing it into gear she tore across the valley as if pursued by all the demons from Hell. She turned up the volume on the stereo.

"...final flight in the dead of night. Destination unknown..."

Kendra stood on an outcropping of rock and watched the sun set over Jared's valley. She pulled out her cell phone and punched in a number. Her call was picked up on the first ring.

"Sir, I didn't find it. I've secured the tracking equipment from the jeep and destroyed it. I'm headed to Denver. There's an off chance that Major Hall may have found the locket. I'm almost sure I had to have dropped it near the waterfall. No sir, it wasn't destroyed in the fire. It is still active." A pause. "Affirmative, sir."

The sound of the door to the waiting room opening brought Phil upright, and he was instantly awake as he saw Kendra walking toward him. There was something different about her now, something he had glimpsed briefly before she jumped in her vehicle and raced away across the valley. She was a woman on a mission.

She wasted no time in coming to the point as she dropped into the chair beside him. "Phil, I need to see Major Hall's personal effects. He may have found—"

"Aren't you even going to ask how he's doing?" Phil growled.

Kendra stared at him, leaned her head against the back of the seat and closed her eyes.

"How is he?" She whispered.

"Still alive, but only just."

Her eyes flew open. "How—what—"

"Besides the smoke and the concussion, he was injected with a slow acting poison. They haven't identified it yet."

Kendra reached for her cell phone again. "Maybe I can help."

Phil stared at her. "You know about the poison?"

Her call was picked up. "Sir, Agent Allen here. I'm at the hospital. Major Hall was injected with a slow acting poison. Could you have my records released and sent here? Maybe they can isolate the antidote from my blood. Thank you, sir." She ended the call and let the phone slip from her fingers.

Phil's mouth had dropped open as he listened to her end of the conversation. Now he caught her arms.

"Are you all right? I—"

Her eyelids fluttered before she focused on him. "Will this ever end?" She got to her feet. "I need for someone to take a blood sample. Get started isolating the antidote. If it's the same—"

Phil slipped an arm around her and turned her toward the door. "You are something else, you know. I can't wait to have you on our team."

Kendra looked up at Phil as the technician withdrew the needle and put a band aid over the puncture.

"I still need to see his personal effects. I'm looking for a small brass locket. It has to be where they hid the transmitter. The chain was broken. I had it in my pocket when we went jogging that first evening at the cabin. It must have fallen out when I went for a swim at the waterfall, but I couldn't find it. Maybe he did."

"And maybe that's why they went after him so forcefully." Phil's voice was grim. "I'll get them for you."

"I'm coming with you."

"The nurse said—" He broke off with a sigh as Kendra stood. "Never mind. Why would you start listening to a mere nurse?"

"Actually, she's a technician."

"And you can't be bothered listening to a technician?"

"Not when it's a matter of life and death."

"Let's go get that locket. He had it in his hand when we got here."

CHAPTER TWELVE

Had it been just over a week ago that she sat across the table from General Starr in this same coffee shop, Kendra asked herself. The only difference today was that Phil was with them. That, and Jared was slowly dying from the poison they had yet to identify.

"Tell me why you are so certain it has to be this locket," General Starr said, turning the object in question back and forth between his fingers.

"Remember I told you something was not quite right, that I was disoriented. I had already ingested the poison, but I didn't know it at the time. My hair was loose, the clasp lying on my desk. When I pushed my hair back, the chain on my locket became tangled and when I managed to free it, the chain was broken. I don't know whether I broke it, or whether someone else did. I never took it off because it was the last gift my brother gave me before—before he was killed." She swallowed and wet her lips. "I never opened it, although there was a picture inside. It was water tight, so I never worried about water damage. It would be the perfect place to hide something like a transmitter—" she paused, "—or a microchip."

Two heads jerked towards her in unison, two pair of eyes riveted to her face. For a moment the silence was absolute.

"Say again." From Phil. The general still stared open-mouthed.

Kendra shrugged. "This has gone on too long and gotten too complicated to be about just a transmitter. What if they wanted to pass along information to someone in this country and used me as the means to do it. They couldn't lose track of me, and I was supposed to be dead within a few days, anyway. The only reason I wasn't is that I developed an allergic reaction to the poison before it progressed too far. As soon as my plane landed back in the states, I went to an emergency room. When they told me about the poison, I contacted you, General Starr, and you know the story from there."

"But why try to kill you if they needed you to complete a mission for them? Or why not just kill you after they recovered the information?"

"And why were they so determined to kill Jared?" Phil said. He looked at the general. "Sorry, sir. Major Hall. They hit him in the head hard enough to cause a concussion—a blow that would have probably killed just about anyone else. They blew his cabin up with him supposedly locked in a store room. They didn't know about the trap door. And just in case, they still inject him with a poison."

"Whatever this is," Kendra said, "they don't intend to leave any witnesses." She looked back at General Starr. "Sir, did we ever establish a connection with SueAnn Talmidge? Is she safe?"

"She's as safe as we can make her. She's back at her job with an assistant who is one of ours. She doesn't know that, by the way." The general shot a quelling glance at both Kendra and Phil. They met his gaze and held it for a moment.

"Understood." They said in unison.

"Agent Allen," General Starr turned back to her. "I understand you are close to Major Hall?"

Kendra cleared her throat. "Close, sir?"

He glared at her. "Involved?"

"Only professionally, sir."

"And emotionally?"

She shrugged. "I might have wanted more from the relationship, but Major Hall is a total professional, sir."

"Agent," the general let his exasperation show. "I'm trying to determine if you need a few days to stay with the Major until he recovers."

Kendra stared at him. She wet her lips. "No, sir," she whispered. "I'm ready for whatever comes next. I want this over."

Jared opened eyes that felt as if they had been sand blasted. His lids fell as shards of light again pierced his brain. He squeezed them together and tried to raise a hand to rub his eyes only to find that he could not move his arms.

"So you're awake, Mr. Hall," a cheery voice said. "If you want to open your eyes again, I'll put some drops in them for you. The doctor said they would be quite dry."

Jared tried to wet lips that felt as dry as his eyes. "The light," he croaked. "Turn off—"

"You want the light off? I'll dim it. I need to see to put the drops in."

Cautiously, Jared slit one eye. Almost instantly, he felt a drop of moisture spread soothingly across the surface. He blinked and opened it wider, felt a drop in the other eye.

"You have the most beautiful eyelashes I have ever seen on a man," the voice went on. "Why isn't some lucky girl doing this for you instead of me?"

Jared focused on the woman behind the voice and recognized the uniform of a volunteer.

"And the eyes are just as beautiful," the voice crooned. "Brown with shards of gold. Most unusual."

Jared couldn't help the grin. "What? You specialize in eyes or something?" he asked.

"Or something," came the saucy reply.

"How long have I been here? What—"

"I rang for your nurse. She will let the doctor know that you've come around. As for how long, this is my third day with you. Your friend had to leave for a couple of days, but he should be getting back today."

"Why can't I move my arms?"

"Probably because of all the IVs. I'm sure the doctor will explain. Ah, here's your nurse now."

"Don't go—"

"I'm just getting out of the way so the nurse can check you. I'll be here when she leaves."

"Thanks."

Jared lay with eyes closed as he felt the nurse check his blood pressure and pulse. He obediently opened his mouth for the thermometer.

"Well, Mr. Hall, your blood pressure has improved greatly over the last few days. It's almost back up to normal."

"Back up to normal?" he echoed.

"Um-huh. You may not know it, but you have been one very sick young man."

"Because of the smoke I inhaled—"

"There was that. Dr. Phillips will be here shortly. He'll fill in the rest."

"Wait—" Jared lay back with a sigh as he heard the nurse bustle from the room. He realized belatedly that he hadn't opened his eyes and looked at her. Except for her voice, he wouldn't even recognize her when she returned.

He felt a gentle hand on his arm. "There, dear. You mustn't get frustrated."

He turned toward the voice, still without opening his eyes. "Did anyone else visit me? A girl—" He broke off. He hadn't meant to ask.

"A girl?"

"Tall, slender, athletic. Dark hair. Gray eyes. You can't miss the gray eyes." He sighed.

"Obviously you do."

Another sigh. "Yeah."

"I haven't seen her, but maybe she comes when I'm not here."

"She hasn't been here," Jared said with certainty. "I would have known."

"That special, huh?"

Jared thought for a moment. "She is. Maybe she finally realizes that I'm not."

"If that's the case, she must be very hard to please." She squeezed his hand. "Here's the doctor, now."

Jared opened his eyes, finding the light marginally less painful now.

"Good afternoon, Major Hall. I'm Dr. Jordan Phillips."

Jared nodded, wondering at the formal use of his rank. He had been retired for years.

"I guess the last thing you probably remember is the explosion and fire." The doctor dropped into a chair beside the bed.

Jared nodded again. "That. And Kendra rescuing me. And a couple of guys. Probably the ones who hit me and blew up the cabin."

"Well, those guys did something else to you. They gave you an injection." The doctor paused.

Jared frowned. "Some kind of drug? I felt rather uncoordinated. Sluggish."

"That could have been from the concussion."

Jared thought about that. "So what are you trying to tell me, doc? What kind of injection?"

"A slow acting poison. Fortunately for you, there had been one other recent case. We were able to identify the drug and administer the antidote."

"One other recent case?" Jared repeated blankly.

"A young lady with military intelligence. She got us started with a blood sample as soon as she heard." He shrugged. "Then she disappeared." The doctor had been making notes as he talked. Now he closed the chart and stood up. "As soon as you feel up to it, you're to call a General Starr. It looks as if you have turned the corner. Welcome back, young man."

Jared turned his head as Phil walked into the room and threw a duffle bag on a table.

"What does Kendra's boss want with me?" Jared asked.

Phil threw him a glance. "Hey, and it's really great to see you, too! Bright eyed and chipper. I'd say the prognosis is that you will live."

Jared narrowed his gaze. "General Starr?"

Phil dropped into a chair. "He did not share that information with me. We did find the transmitter in the brass locket you had in your hand. The last I heard, they were doing some tests on it."

"On the transmitter?"

"And the locket. Kendra seems to think there is more involved than a mere transmitter."

"More like what?"

"Sorry. After I handed over his agent, the general politely thanked me for my time and showed me the door. I've talked to Kendra a couple of times, but apparently my security clearance isn't up to par."

"So, I repeat, what does the general want with a beat up ex-Special Forces major?"

"I don't think he recognizes the ex-part. I think he may have a job for the whole group."

"Doesn't he know I'm retired?"

"Are you? If our national security is at stake—"

"He has people like Kendra to handle that."

"And when people like Kendra get captured by some ego-maniacal madman?"

Jared sighed. "Did you bring me some clothes?"

"Clothes. Toothbrush. You name it. When can I spring you?"

"As soon as I've talked with the general. I wanted to see what you knew before I called him. What do we know about this poison? What kind of side effects, after effects, whatever, can I expect?"

Phil shrugged. "Your guess is as good as mine. Kendra's case unfolded quite differently than yours. She had the poison in her body longer than you have before she even knew it. But she had already started to reject it. They were able to build on that to develop an antidote. Apparently blood types respond in different ways."

Jared sighed. "Do we have a clue yet what these nutcases want? Besides me dead, that is."

"Kendra and the general are working on that. Our orders are merely to stand by."

Kendra stared at the mock-up projected on the wall of the conference room where everyone who was anyone with DIA had gathered..

"Have you figured out what you're looking at, Agent?" The question was barked at her from a grizzled looking gentleman in a scruffy lab coat.

"The entire Region One power grid shut down, which means that a couple dozen nuclear plants will go to fail-safe mode and shut down. It will take days if not weeks to bring them back on line, and meantime, our entire center of trade, commerce and government is affected."

"*If* we can bring them back up," General Matthew Starr stood at the back of the room. "We have reason to believe, Agent, that the nuclear power plants are the target. We sent you on this mission to try and trace the destination of several missing shipments of plutonium. We now believe that they never left this country, and that they will be used on site at several of these plants to initiate explosions. Not only will the entire eastern seaboard be without power, it will be uninhabitable for several thousand years."

A stunned silence filled the room for a micro-second or so.

"What are we doing about this, sir?" Kendra asked.

In spite of the gravity of the situation, Matthew Starr could not help the twitch at the corner of his mouth. Leave it to his top agent to cut straight to the heart of the matter.

"We have agents embedded in all these locations. Thanks to you, we now have times and dates. We can move forward with preventive measures."

"That's not good enough, sir."

Having expected this response, the general had to fight to hold back a grin. Agent Allen seldom disappointed him.

"Agent, I know you want to see this mission through—"

"I will see this mission through, sir."

"Not without backup, you won't."

"Sorry, sir. I don't do backup. You know I work alone."

"Not this time, Agent." The general's mouth tightened. Sometimes, however, he had to disappoint Agent Allen. "Meet me in my office when we adjourn."

CHAPTER THIRTEEN

Kendra sucked in a deep breath and closed her eyes, her fists clenched at her sides. "Sir, I cannot work with Major Hall." She enunciated each word carefully.

"Why not?" Matthew Starr asked. "It seems he's gotten you out of tight spots a couple of times. You make a great team."

"Right. Thanks to me, he's almost gotten killed at least three times in the past two weeks."

"But you were there to save him each time. Like I said, you make a great team."

Kendra sank into a chair, all the fight draining out of her. "I'm not going to win this one, am I, sir?" she asked, her voice heavy with defeat.

"I can't afford to let you. You're too valuable to risk, but I have to let you go through with this mission. Major Hall is my ace in the hole."

"I wish you would reconsider, sir. I've never used back up."

"You will never know that he's around."

Kendra smiled at that. She shook her head. "Trust me, sir. I would know if Jared Hall is in the next county."

"And he is just as aware of you. I'm counting on that to give us an edge." He picked up the locket lying on his desk. "We have made a few modifications, including repairing the chain so that you can wear this again. The only thing you have to do is let them find you."

Kendra suppressed a shudder. "Understood, sir."

"We have added our own little tracking device, both for Major Hall's benefit, and for when our friends recover their microchip. All the information on it is intact."

The general paused before pushing a watch across the desk. "We have added a transmitter to your watch. We think they will snatch the locket and run, but in case they decide to take you along, we have no intention of losing track of you."

Kendra slid the watch over her hand and settled it around her wrist. "Gee, sir, you don't know how safe that makes me feel." He did not miss the flash in her gray eyes.

General Starr sighed and drummed his fingers on his desk. Kendra held her breath as a frown creased his brow. Had she pushed too far?

"All right, Agent. Let's have it. Suppose I let you go in alone. How would you handle it?"

Kendra stared at him as she let the words sink in. Slowly a smile lit her face. "How would I handle it, sir?" She repeated. "You know how well I know this case. This is what I would do…"

"He what?" Jared turned from his packing to pin Phil with a glare. "He's decided to send her in without backup after all. He can't do that!"

"I'm afraid he can," Phil said. "He not only has three stars, that he earned himself, by the way. No political promotions here. He happens to be head of the DIA. He can do whatever he chooses with an agent."

Jared continued to glare at him until Phil squirmed. "She insisted, Jared. She's always worked alone. She didn't want backup."

"Didn't want backup—or didn't want me?" Jared sank down on the side of the bed.

"I don't imagine it helped that her backup was you. She blames herself for the fact that you were almost killed. She—"

"She has quite an over-developed sense of responsibility," Jared said bitterly. "If she still carries around the guilt of her brother's death, of course she would blame herself for any imagined threat to anyone she knows."

"You aren't just anyone, and the threats were hardly imagined."

"Neither were they her fault." Jared got up to pace. "So where does that leave us?"

"Still on stand-by," Phil replied.

Jared raised a brow in question.

"General Starr agreed to let her go in alone. He did not promise not to send back up if he deems it necessary."

A brief smile lightened Jared's features. "I may learn to like this General Starr!"

"There's something that keeps bothering me," Phil said as he paced the room. "Kendra doesn't think these people plan to leave any witnesses."

Jared's head jerked up. "What does that mean?"

"Just something she said when we were talking about all their attempts to neutralize you. And who knows them better than she does?"

"So she went back in—" Jared swallowed and reached for the back of a chair for support. "She went back in knowing that there's a good chance she won't come out again."

"Isn't that the case with all her assignments," Phil pointed out. "However, this time, she thinks this has gone on too long, there's too much at stake, and she's the only one who stands a chance of stopping them in time."

Jared dropped into a chair. "I'm beginning to understand that 99 percent of the male population who find her intimidating. She's a machine." His tone held no admiration.

"Hardly," Phil said dryly. "There's a very good chance this will be her last mission. She's had enough—"

"It very well could be," Jared grated. "Not the way you mean, but it very well could be."

Kendra wandered idly through the subway station, all her sense on alert. It stood to reason that her quarry would have tracked the locket to Washington, and that by now they would know she had it on her person. All she had to do was wait to be approached. She dropped some coins into a vending machine and selected a canned soda. Pretending to sip from it, she let her eyes scan the surrounding area.

Possibly not the best location she could have chosen, she admitted now that it was too late. The mall area around the Washington Monument might just be the world's largest melting pot. How was she to filter out someone speaking German when she had heard at least a dozen different languages already? She sank onto a bench and checked her watch, pretending to wait for her train.

A heavy body landed on the bench beside her with a thud and before she could register the significance, a large hand locked around her wrist and another reached for her throat, seizing the locket around her neck.

"Ah, *Freulein*, but you have led me on a wild bird chase, is it not? Regretfully, for you, you have failed." He jerked the locket and Kendra heard a tiny *ting* that was the transmitter concealed inside the locket being activated by the breaking chain. He dropped the locket into a pocket and zipped it closed.

"We have decided to let you live. It will be for such a short time, surely it is not worth while to neutralize you." He stared at her for a moment, and something akin to admiration flashed in his eyes. He shrugged. "Besides, it would be a crime to eliminate so worthy an opponent."

Kendra stared at him, belatedly realizing that she had a role to play.

"My locket," she said huskily, her hand going to her throat. "What do you want with my locket—?"

"Silence!" In a flash his eyes were cold and deadly. "Do not ask questions, *Freulein*. Just be grateful for your life—miserably short time that you have." He whirled away from her and disappeared into the milling throng.

Kendra sprang into action. She slung her bag over her shoulder and headed toward a bank of pay phones. Wouldn't the logical thing to do after an assault be to call the police? At least that would be what anyone who might be watching would assume she would do.

"She did it." Matthew Starr replaced the receiver and raked a hand through his hair. "She heard the transmitter being activated and our agents are following it as we speak. She is going to disappear for awhile."

"They let her go." Jared Hall leaned over the General's desk. "Just like that."

The General shrugged. "Didn't feel it was necessary to kill her." Suddenly the weight of the world that he literally carried on his shoulders seemed too much and he slumped in his chair. "All of us have such a short time, according to her assailant, that it wasn't worth his time to neutralize her." He looked up to meet Jared's eyes. "She has done her job, Major. Now it is up to the rest of us to save our civilization."

"What do you need me to do, sir?"

The general pushed a small tracking device across the desk. "I believe she knows to head west, although no one knows how far she should go. I told her about the transmitter in her watch, but I doubt she will remember, at least not right away. That's all I can do for you, Major. Good luck."

Kendra flashed her turn signal and exited the highway for a truck stop she had visited a couple of times. She needed food and caffeine, not necessarily in that order. She hadn't slept in almost forty-eight hours. She pulled into a slot between two huge tractor-trailer rigs and headed toward the bright lights of the all night café.

A car screeched into a parking space beside her. Before she could gather her wits to turn and flee, the door flew open and a slender woman with long brown hair erupted from the car.

"Kendra Allen, as I live and breathe! Where have you been? You are the last person I would have expected to run into, but the first I would have chosen."

Kendra stared at her, trying to pull her scattered thoughts into focus. "TJ?"

"Sure! All grown up now, just like you." Terri Jo Parker linked her arm with Kendra's. "Are you headed for the restaurant? May I join you?"

Unable to even begin to keep pace with her vivacious friend's line of chatter, Kendra could only nod. She let herself be led inside and over to a booth. A waitress dropped off menus and filled Kendra's cup with coffee. Terri put her hand over her cup.

"Do you have any hot tea?" she asked the waitress.

"'Fraid not."

"Then a glass of water please. No ice."

After they placed their order, Terri sat for a moment staring at Kendra, as if it had finally dawned on her that her friend was perhaps too quiet.

"I know it's been a long time," Terri begin, "but you look—" she paused, searching for the right word.

"About done in. On my last legs. On the verge of collapse." Kendra sipped her coffee. "All of the above."

It was Terri's turn to find her self at a loss for words.

"So, you might ask, what have I been doing with myself?" Kendra said. "How about saving the world from nuclear annihilation? Or maybe fighting a losing battle to preserve western civilization? Or it could just be falling in love with the wrong man—or at the very least, the right man at the wrong time." She drained her coffee and motioned to the waitress. "So what brings you to this virtually uninhabited corner of the planet? You do still live in Houston, right?"

Terri nodded and found her voice. "I've been visiting my brother in California. I'm on my way home. School starts next week. I still work as a high school counselor, although I'm not sure how much longer I can continue."

"I think your job might be a little bit tougher than mine," Kendra said. "I can't imagine why you do it."

"In my way, I'm also working to preserve western civilization," Terri said quietly.

Kendra studied her. "I guess you are, at that." She stared into her cup for a moment. "You remind me of someone I met a long time ago. Someone who made a major difference in my life. That would be the kind of job you could really get your teeth into."

"Tell me more."

"It's a youth camp called 'Camp Sunrise', run by a guy named Michael Braden. It's a last chance program for kids like the one I used to be—the ones that parents, counselors, even society, can no longer reach."

"I may have to check into it." Terri sipped her water. "Now tell me more about this guy you've gone over the edge for," she said, her eyes dancing. "I always thought you would be the last one to fall. He must be something else entirely."

"Oh, he's all that," Kendra said. "Trust me."

CHAPTER FOURTEEN

Kendra pulled her Bronco into a parking space before the large metal hangar and sat for a moment, numb and exhausted. After leaving Terri at the diner west of Denver, she had driven straight through to Holland Aviation north of San Francisco. She had called ahead to charter a plane that would fly her the rest of the way to her destination.

She reached for the door handle and saw the watch still on her wrist.

"We have added a transmitter to your watch. We think they will snatch the locket and run, but in case they decide to take you along, we have no intention of losing track of you."

"Well, that's over," Kendra grumbled. She slid the watch off her wrist and threw it on the dash, then stepped out of the vehicle. A tall man with dark hair strode across the tarmac toward her.

Kendra paused and briefly remembered the first time she had seen Matt Walker during Operation Desert Storm in Kuwait. It had been her first assignment and he was a brand new A-10 pilot. No one looked better in uniform than he did. As they became friends, she quickly realized that some lucky woman had already claimed his heart. No one was more surprised than she to learn that said lucky woman was one of her best friends, Kris Holland.

"Kendra," Matt's voice was husky as he caught her in a quick embrace. "I know you said you were in a hurry, but you can't possibly think you'll get away without saying 'Hi' to Kris."

"Kris," Kendra repeated blankly. "Is she here?"

He looked at her. "Is it possible that you missed the news that we got married?"

She stared at him. "When?"

He grinned. "The day after we ran into you at the airport in San Francisco last year. Come on. You have to see Kris. We have a surprise for you."

"No, Matt, really—"

"Kendra! Matt said you were coming."

Kendra turned at the sound of the voice to see one of her oldest friends coming toward her, although not very quickly. It took a moment for the reason to register. Her eyes flew to Matt.

"Matt! Kris! You're—you're having a baby!" She flew across the ramp to catch Kris in her arms. "When? What? Oh, I'm so happy for you!"

Matt caught up to them and swung an arm around his wife's shoulders. "Come on inside, Kendra. You have to take time for a glass of tea. And tell me again where I'm flying you. I'm not so sure about all this."

"So what have you been doing with yourself?" Kris asked as she placed a glass of tea in front of Kendra. "You look—" she paused to consider her words. "Exhausted is the only word that fits."

Kendra sighed and took a long drink of the tea, her mouth twisting into a smile as she remembered a similar exchange with Terri Parker. "You don't know the half of it." She looked around. "Have you heard any news lately? Anything major going on?"

Matt's eyes narrowed as he watched her. "Should there be?"

"I hope so. But we may not hear about it for awhile." She looked up as Kris put a plate of cookies and sandwiches in front of her. "Kris, you're a life saver. How did you know I was starving?"

"When have you ever not been starving?" Kris grinned.

Matt sat down across from her and stretched out his long legs. "So tell me about this place where you want to go."

"Actually, it's my home. I bought it a few years ago and I've been working on it, getting it ready for when I retire."

"Has that happened?" Matt asked quietly, hopefully.

Kendra gave a sharp nod, unable to speak. Suddenly her eyes filled with tears and a lump blocked her throat. "I can't—" her voice broke and she brought a hand to cover her mouth.

"Kendra!" Kris dropped down beside her, putting an arm around her to draw her close.

"I can't do that kind of work anymore, Matt!" Kendra sobbed. "I can't—"

He caught her hand and squeezed it gently. "You don't know how glad I am to hear that," he said. "Between the two of us, we've kept God working overtime for way too long." His mouth twisted. "To say nothing of our friends in Special Forces."

"I feel like—there's nothing left. I don't know who I am without my work. I have to get away for awhile until I figure it out."

"Maybe, but not until you get some rest," Dr. Kris Holland ordered. "You're spending the night and Matt will fly you wherever you need to go tomorrow."

"But, I can't—"

"There's no point in arguing," Matt grinned. "You'll be just fine unless she offers you warm milk. Avoid it like the plague."

Kris wrinkled her nose at him. "Warm milk is the cure for most ills. But I know that Kendra can't drink milk. I'll have to think of something else."

Kendra suddenly slumped from exhaustion. "You know, I could use a little rest, if I'm not too much trouble."

"No trouble at all," Kris assured her as she stood. "Just eat a few bites while I go find some clean towels and pajamas."

"Before you go, guess who I ran into—I can't remember—yesterday, or the day before." She bit into a cookie.

Kris shook her head. "I have no idea."

"TJ Parker."

"TJ?" Kris's eyes widened. "I haven't kept up with her since we all met that summer. How is she?"

"Not doing too much better than I am. Burned out. I'm worried about her. She gives too much of herself to her job."

Matt made a sound of disgust. "Well, if anyone would know about that, it would be you."

156

Kendra glared at him. "Look at the pot calling the kettle black," she growled.

"Children! Children!" Kris admonished. When she had their attention, she grinned. "Thank you. Now, we've all been there. Me, maybe even more than either of you. But it is possible to change things. Matt has, and so have I. Tell us more about this place you're going to. What are you planning to do?"

Kendra finished her cookie and picked up a sandwich. "I have a partner. We're breeding and training therapy and working dogs."

Kris dropped back into her chair. "Kendra, that's perfect for you. I remember how much you love animals." Her mouth twisted. "As opposed to people, for instance. Who is this partner?"

"He's a veterinary student—a lot younger than me, named Timothy Matthews. He used to be a neighbor kid." She swallowed with difficulty. "We've—stayed in touch. When he found out I intended to do this, he wanted to help out. He has a friend who is a trainer. We have a dozen dogs now, the first litter almost finished with their training. An older couple has been living on the property to keep it up and take care of the dogs when one of us can't be there. I think it's time I do this. I've thought about it for a long time."

"Then go for it. It sounds like the time is right and you have done a lot of planning," Matt said. "The only thing I'm curious about is why I have to fly you there."

"I could drive, but this will save me a lot of time. I only have a few days left to make a decision concerning my service with the DIA. I want to make the most of that time. I hope I can decide to resign."

"What would cause you to decide otherwise?" Kris asked.

"I have to know that raising and training dogs will be enough for me. I've lived—" Kendra paused, again trying to find the right word.

157

"On the edge?" Kris suggested dryly.

Kendra nodded. "You could say that. I never felt I had a reason to want anything more. But now—" she hesitated.

"Have you met someone, Kendra?" Kris asked.

Kendra met her gaze. "Why would you ask that?"

"Maybe I recognize the symptoms."

Kendra sighed. "Yes, I've met someone. Someone who is perfect for me, but I'm all wrong for him. Knowing me has almost gotten Jared killed several times in the last few weeks."

"Jared?" Matt repeated. "As in Major Jared Hall, perhaps?"

Kendra raised her head to stare at him. "How—how could you possibly know that?"

"You wrote that you were going to sign up for an Extreme Expedition," Kris said. "I went on one a couple of years ago and met Jared. Matt knows Major Hall and remembered that his unit rescued your team in Kuwait. We thought—well, we wondered how the two of you would get along, considering your history and all."

Kendra studied her for a moment. "Considering my history," she said thoughtfully. "It always comes down to that, doesn't it?"

Kendra looked down at the terrain below them as Matt circled to come in for a landing at an airstrip a couple of miles from Kendra's property. They had flown over it and she had not seen anyone around.

"You're sure you'll be okay?" Matt asked again as he helped her unload her bags. "That's quite a hike you have to get there."

"I'll be fine. I have a truck here. I have phone service. The place should be well stocked with food. I'm sure that Mr. and Mrs. Woods have just gone into town for a few hours. I didn't call to let them know I was coming."

"Will you call me and let me know that all is well as soon as you get there? If I'm not back, leave a message with Kris. And if you need me to come back for you, just call. Will you do that?"

Kendra looked at him for a moment, then reached up to kiss him on the cheek. "I forgot to tell Kris how lucky she is," she said with a grin.

"Actually, I'm the lucky one," Matt growled. "I'll never know what she sees in me."

Kendra stared at him. "Maybe you don't, at that." She gave a sharp salute. "Thanks. I'll keep in touch."

"You do that."

Jared pulled into the drive of the modest suburban home and cut his engine. He sat deep in thought for a moment.

The door to the house burst open and a man about his age and build ran down the steps. Jared stepped out of the car to meet him.

"Jared, buddy, it was good to hear from you. I'd say you were a sight for sore eyes, except—" Michael Braden stopped talking for a moment to study Jared. "Frankly, you look like death warmed over."

"And feel about the same," Jared confessed. "Thanks, Mike, for making time for me. The last few weeks have been—rather difficult."

"Come inside before you collapse in my drive. I'll whip up some lunch for us and you can tell me all about it."

Jared followed his old friend inside, barely making it to the kitchen where he collapsed onto a barstool, sweat beading his forehead.

"Man," Michael studied him again. "Did you pick up some kind of bug? You look weak as a kitten."

"Try thallium poisoning."

Michael Braden stared at him, slowly sinking onto a barstool himself. "Talk to me, Jared. Did I hear you say thallium?"

"I'm out of danger. They don't even think my hair will fall out. They had the antidote within hours, but it takes the body a while to rebuild itself."

"So how did this happen?"

"One of your former graduates works for the DIA."

"You wouldn't be talking about Kendra Allen?"

Jared sighed. "Who else?"

Michael drew a deep breath. "Don't tell me she gave you the poison?"

Jared stared at him. "Of course not. She was the first one to receive it. She saved my life by helping to identify the poison right away."

"So who was behind these attempted murders?"

Jared shrugged. "As far as I know, that information is still classified. But that's not what I need to talk to you about."

"It's not?" The stunned expression on Michael Braden's face would have been comical if Jared had had the strength to laugh.

"I need you to tell me everything you can remember about Kendra. I have to be able to get through to her—reach her—help her. Mike, I know we never thought it could happen, but I'm almost sure—" he paused.

"Yes?" Michael prodded when Jared did not continue.

Jared shrugged. "I'm in love with her. I have to find a way to get her off this track she's on."

"And what track is that?"

"A fast track to destruction. I think she knows, but she doesn't care. She has no reason to care. I have to try and give her one."

Michael drummed his fingers on the counter for a moment. "Kendra was the most damaged child I've ever met. That's easy to understand considering what happened to her brother. Her parents didn't do anything wrong that I can see. She just—the best I can figure out, a part of her died that day as well. The miracle is that she has figured out a way to function at all.

"I know it was hard on you when Amanda died. I know you still blame yourself that you weren't there to take care of her. It was hard for me when my cousin was killed in that drive by shooting. I blamed myself for ever letting him get near a gang—which he wouldn't have done if I hadn't been involved. Those were major life defining moments for us as well, but we were older. We had some control over what we did with our lives from that moment on.

"Kendra didn't have that kind of control. She was still dependent on others—her parents whose lives she felt she had destroyed as well. Her teachers whom she thought looked at her as a murderer. Her friends, whose parents would no longer let them sleep over at her house."

Jared looked at Michael. "Kendra described herself as coming close to being your first failure. Is that accurate?"

Michael shrugged. "I was still pretty new at this business. Let's just say we used about every trick in my bag."

"Is there anything you would do different if you had her in your program now?"

"Pray a lot more, ask for help from a Higher Source. The only one who can help Kendra, in the end, will be Kendra. She has to want to be different. And when she has a reason to live again, she will be afraid again."

161

"What do you mean?"

"She has no fear because she has no reason to live. When she has that reason again, she will not be willing to take the kind of chances we know she takes. We can only pray that happens soon."

Jared stared at Michael for a long moment. "If I need help, will it be okay if I call you? I'm not sure I can do this alone."

"Pray about it, my friend. You won't be alone." Michael reached out to clasp Jared's shoulder. "But go ahead and call me. If you need me, I'll be there the quickest way possible." He looked thoughtful for a moment. "Kendra was special, and I don't like to leave a job unfinished."

CHAPTER FIFTEEN

Jared punched a number into his cell phone and pushed the send button. A moment later, he heard a familiar voice.

"Mr. Allen, this is Jared Hall. I don't know if you remember me—"

"Of course I remember you, Major. What can I do for you?"

"I wondered if you know where Kendra is—or might be?"

"Well, she called a few days ago. Didn't want us to worry about her? She was on her way to California—San Francisco. Hold on a second—"

Jared listened to a slight rustling sound for a few seconds, afraid to hope this might be the lead he needed.

"Here it is," Jim Allen returned to the phone. "Holland Aviation. Says she has friends there and was going to charter a plane to fly up to a cabin she owns. If I needed to reach her, they would know how."

"Thank you, sir. You don't know how much this means to me."

"Maybe I do," Jim said agreeably. "Good luck, Major."

Jared ended the call and dropped his phone into his pocket. *Holland Aviation*. Small world, but then considering he was still in Colorado, maybe not so small after all.

Kendra reached the cabin and knocked on the door. After waiting several minutes and getting no answer, she looked around for the spare key. She pushed the door open and stepped inside, fumbling for a light switch.

It only took a few seconds to assure herself that the house was empty. She found a phone number scrawled by the phone and hesitated a few seconds before dialing it.

"I'm trying to find Mr. and Mrs. Abel Woods," she said to the voice on the other end of the line.

"One moment, please."

A sound of the receiver being laid down, then picked up.

"Abel Woods here."

"Mr. Woods," Kendra sounded breathless and forced her self to slow down. "This is Kendra Allen. I just got to the cabin—"

"Kendra, love. I'm sorry we aren't there. Molly fell this morning. It doesn't seem to be too serious, but they're still checking her out."

"What doesn't seem to be too serious?" Kendra asked.

"Her injuries. She has a sprained ankle and probably a sprained wrist, but nothing seems to be broken."

"That's good news. So where are you now?"

"I drove over to my brother's place. They want to keep Molly overnight, so I thought I would stay in town. I left plenty of food for the dogs and Jenna will be there in the morning."

"Don't worry about that," Kendra assured him. "I'll be here for a while. I'll take care of everything. Give Molly my love and tell her I'll keep her in my prayers."

Kendra hung up the phone and dropped down onto a stool.

"In case it's important, I don't cook."

"Then you'll learn."

A smile touched Kendra's mouth, then faded. *Too bad they hadn't finished the program.* She was starving, but her culinary skills didn't even run to scrambled eggs. She could only hope she would find some fruit or crackers.

She stood. That would have to wait. She needed to check on the dogs before it got any later.

As expected, the dogs greeted her cautiously, but without malicious intent. It took almost half an hour to regain their trust. She filled food and water bowls and shook out bedding. By the time she closed the kennel, she had barely enough light left to make her way back to the house. Thunder rumbled to the northwest and an occasional flash of lightning revealed an ominous buildup of clouds.

Kendra checked the pantry and refrigerator. She found a can of soup and eventually unearthed a can opener. She set out a box of graham crackers to save for breakfast. If Abel and Molly didn't return tomorrow, she would run over to the nearest town and pick up the kind of food she knew how to prepare for herself.

As she cleaned up the kitchen, Kendra heard lightning strike nearby and almost instantly the power went out. She stood frozen. She hadn't yet thought to look for a flashlight or lantern. The best she could remember, they were in a drawer under the sink. Feeling her way, she edged along the counter. The second drawer she checked contained a flashlight, batteries and a first aid kit. She took them into the den and curled up on the sofa, pulling a cotton throw over herself. Rain pelted against the window, and wind shook the small cabin. She closed her eyes and burrowed into the pillow as sleep claimed her.

Jared peered ahead through his rain lashed windshield. No use trying to continue in this storm. He needed to find a place to pull over and wait out the storm. He'd just passed a sign for a roadside park if he could manage to find the turnoff. A gust of wind caught his Jeep and he fought to keep it on the road. He saw the exit and eased into it. The parking area was deserted and only a couple of security lights provided illumination. Even as he watched, they flickered and went out, plunging the area into total darkness. He cut his ignition and turned off the lights, listening to the sound of rain lashing against his frail vehicle and feeling the gusts of wind that caught at it. Good thing he'd stopped for dinner a couple of hours back. He wouldn't be going anywhere for a while.

Kendra straightened and wiped sweat from her forehead. She had cleared most of the limbs that the storm blew down and had managed to call and get power restored. Jenna had called to say she couldn't get over because a fallen tree was blocking the road. So much for getting into town for supplies.

Kendra threw the chain saw and a can of fuel in the back of the beat up truck that served as transportation for who ever happened to need it. Might as well see if she could tackle that tree before she went inside and cleaned up.

A couple of hours later she had completed as much of the job as she could do alone and Kendra climbed back into the truck. Exhaustion dragged at her. By the time she reached the cabin, she barely found the energy to get out of the truck and walk inside. She should be starving, but had no appetite, which was actually a good thing, considering. She took a quick shower and shrugged into a robe, then went into the guest room and lay down across the bed. She couldn't remember ever feeling this bad. *Except once.* Just after she returned from that last mission. *Just before she found out she had been injected with thallium.*

"Matt's not here. May I help you?"

Jared closed the door to his Jeep and turned to see a vaguely familiar man in his early fifties.

"Hey, I know you." The man grinned and held out his hand. "Bret Brown, chief pilot. And you're the guy who keeps trying to hire Matt to fly charters for your company."

Jared nodded. "Jared Hall. Actually, I need a charter now. I believe Matt flew a friend of mine to a cabin a few days ago. I'm supposed to follow, but I don't exactly know how to get there."

"Matt will be away for a day or two. Kris went into labor last night and he took her to the hospital."

"I heard they got married and Kris was expecting. I guess I didn't realize it was already time for her to deliver. Well, that's great news!"

Bret studied him. "I might be able to help you. If you know which plane he used to fly the charter for your friend, I can pull up the GPS record and probably deliver you to the same spot on the map."

"I'm afraid I don't know what plane—wouldn't he keep a log?"

"Most likely. It may take a few minutes to pull up the information. The office is this way if you want to get something to drink."

Jared shoved his hands into his pockets and absently felt the tracking device that Matthew Starr had given him. Unconsciously, he pressed the button to activate it and almost tripped when it began beeping. He stopped and pulled the receiver from his pocket.

Bret had turned to look at him. "What is that?"

"There's a transmitter on my friend's car. It seems to be around here somewhere." He scanned the parking area as he spoke.

"A burgundy Bronco, maybe?" Bret asked.

"Sounds right."

"It's in the hangar over here and that probably means this is the plane Matt used. Just let me check and—are you interested in leaving right away?"

"As soon as possible. I'd like to get there tonight. Do we have enough daylight left?"

"Depends on where we're going. Let me check on those coordinates and I'll be right back."

While Bret did a pre-flight and got the plane ready to fly, Jared returned to the Jeep and grabbed his duffle bag. Was it possible that he might see Kendra again tonight? It felt like a lifetime since he had last seen her—since she had saved his life for the second time. She had saved it again a third time by knowing about the thallium poisoning, but he had not seen her then. Nor had she visited him in the hospital.

Somehow he didn't think Matt Walker would be as willing to fly this charter as Bret seemed to be. He didn't know whether Kendra might have sworn Matt to secrecy, but he had been prepared to use any means of coercion necessary to gain Matt's cooperation. Maybe his luck had turned.

Yeah, right, his luck had turned, Jared told himself in disgust a few hours later as he watched the blue and white Cessna disappear into the setting sun. He had at least a two mile hike to the cabin they had flown over—the one he assumed must be Kendra's. He frowned. It had looked deserted except for an abandoned truck out front. Had he just made a major tactical error?

Kendra awakened with a burning thirst. Her body felt as if it were on fire. She stripped off the robe and pulled on a T-shirt and sweat pants and walked barefoot into the kitchen for a glass of water. She flipped on a light and got a glass from the cabinet.

A pounding on the back door startled her and the glass slipped from her fingers, shattering on the polished wood floor. She felt a sting of pain and looked down to see a shard of glass embedded in the top of her foot. The pounding came again.

"Kendra, are you in there? This is Jared."

She stared at the door. *Jared?* That was not possible. She was hallucinating. *Somehow she had been poisoned again!*

She looked down at the shards of broken glass surrounding her bare feet and the blood pooling on top of her foot. Her fists clenched in helpless frustration as she tried to swallow the fear threatening to overwhelm her. The pounding came again.

"No!" The cry tore from her throat.

CHAPTER SIXTEEN

Without stopping to think, Jared dropped his duffle bag and rammed his shoulder against the door. He heard the sound of splintering wood and found himself lying on the floor looking up at Kendra.

"Are you all right?" he asked. "I heard a scream."

She stared at him, her eyes wide and dilated in her flushed face. She stabbed her fingers into her hair.

"Jared? Is that you? Am I *not* hallucinating?"

He got to his feet. "Well, I'm here. Why would you think you were hallucinating?" He started toward her.

"Be careful," she said. "I broke a glass and I have a cut—"

He glanced down to see the deadly shards of glass surrounding her bare feet and the blood oozing from the cut she had already suffered. He felt his heart thump painfully.

"Kendra, love," he said huskily. He scooped her up and set her on the counter. "Stay put while I get rid of this broken glass." He looked around for a broom and dust pan.

"Now I know I'm hallucinating," Kendra said as she watched him meticulously sweep up every sliver of glass..

"Oh?" Jared emptied the dust pan into the trash. "Have you never seen a man use a broom before?"

"Only in my dreams."

Jared shook his head as he returned the cleaning supplies to the closet, refusing to be baited. "Do you have a first aid kit?"

She nodded toward a drawer. "How—how are you going to get the glass out?" she asked in a small voice.

He studied her. Was blood something else she was afraid of? That would make sense. Was that what had prompted her scream a moment ago?

"Well," he replied, "if it's too deep, I may have to take you to an emergency room."

"Good luck. There isn't an emergency room for a hundred miles and I didn't get the road cleared."

"Then I guess I will have to see how much medic stuff I remember," he grinned. "It doesn't look like it nicked anything vital. There isn't too much blood." Then he remembered her cry. "Are you afraid of blood, Kendra? Did you scream because you were cut?"

"I—no, that isn't why I screamed. When I heard your voice—well, I thought I had been poisoned again."

He stared at her. "Why would you think that?"

"Because I thought I was hallucinating again, like before I found out

171

about the poison. I already had all the other symptoms. But you're here." She reached up to touch his face. "So maybe not—"

He caught her hand, surprised at how warm it felt, and folded it inside his. "What other symptoms?" he asked.

She plucked at her T-shirt. "I'm hot and thirsty and I'm not hungry. I should be starving because there's no food here and I can't cook—"

Jared touched her forehead and a frown creased his brow. "You do feel awfully warm."

Kendra sighed. "That feels good. Your hands are nice and cool."

He reached into a drawer and pulled out a cloth which he wet and began sponging her face and neck.

"Do you have a thermometer? We'll find out if you have a temperature and how high."

"I don't know." She took the cloth and pressed it against her throat. "It could be in the bathroom. I don't remember one in the first aid kit."

Jared picked her up again and carried her down the hall to set her on the edge of the bed. "Stay put," he said again. "We still have to take care of that glass."

"See if you can find some aspirin," she called as he left the room.

"Can you take acetaminophen?" his voice came back muffled.

"Why? Is that the only thing you can find?"

He stuck his head around the door, a bottle in his hand. "Because you said you haven't eaten. You shouldn't take aspirin on an empty stomach."

"I can take it—the acetaminostuff." She lay back and pulled a pillow under her head.

172

"Good girl." He bent over the bed and pushed the thermometer under her tongue. "Just hold that for a second—" As he talked he reached down and grasped the shard of glass with a pair of tongs and pulled it out. He pressed a gauze pad over the wound and sat down on the side of the bed, raising her injured foot to rest in his lap. "All done. When it stops bleeding I'll put some antibiotic ointment and a band aid on it."

"Jarweed—" She tried to talk around the thermometer and he shook his head and grinned, glancing at his watch.

"Okay, now." He plucked the thermometer from her mouth and read it, his frown returning.

"Not good, huh?" She said, watching his expression.

"We'll see. I'll go find something for you to drink so you can take the acetaminophen. How long have you been feeling like this?"

"Since some time this afternoon. I thought I was just exhausted from cleaning up after the storm, and maybe I needed to eat something. Then I stopped being hungry and started aching."

"It sounds like a virus."

She rested her forehead against her arm. "It sounds like thallium poisoning."

Jared stared at her, heard the fear in her voice. "Let's get you taken care of, then I'll make a couple of phone calls, okay?"

She nodded, raised her head to look at him and tried to focus. "If I'm not hallucinating, what are you doing here?" A tiny frown knit her brow.

Jared grinned. "We'll talk about that later. I'll be right back."

Back in the kitchen Jared found a can of frozen juice in the freezer and ran water over it to thaw it enough to reconstitute it. He poured a glass for

Kendra and shook a couple of pills into his hand. When he returned to the bedroom Kendra still lay as he had left her, with her foot elevated and her eyes closed. He dropped down on the bed beside her.

"Kendra."

She turned her head toward his voice and opened her eyes, then sat up and reached for the glass of juice.

"Where did you find that?" she asked, her eyes wide.

"In the freezer where you would expect to find frozen juice." He quirked an eyebrow and gave her a quizzical look.

After she took a couple of sips, he handed her the pills and watched as she swallowed them.

"Now drink the rest of the juice," he said. "And you might explain why you thought there was no food and you were starving to death."

She drained the glass. Shrugged one shoulder. "I—can't cook. Not even a little bit. I was actually kinda hoping that would be part of the agenda, and then the cougar—" She shivered and reached for a blanket.

Jared reached out to tuck the blanket around her. "Try and get some rest. I'll bring some more juice a little later. Do you have a computer here, and some kind of internet service?"

She looked at him through her lashes. "Of course. What do you take us for out here? Uncivilized? I have a satellite connection. There's a small office off the den. The computer is on a desk in the corner. It isn't a very sophisticated system—no passwords or anything. It should start right up."

"Will you be all right for a few minutes?"

"Of course. Considering I still don't know if you're real—" Her eyes closed and her voice trailed off.

174

Jared looked at her for a moment. "I'm as real as you want me to be, my love," he whispered and then he turned away and went in search of the computer.

His mouth twisted wryly. *Not a very sophisticated system* was an understatement, he realized, as he recognized the same outdated set-up he used at home. A phone sat on the desk and he picked it up and dialed a number while he waited for the system to power up.

"Dr. Phillips," Jared said when his call was picked up. "I need some information on thallium poisoning symptoms."

Jared returned to the bedroom and found it empty. He checked the bathroom and called to Kendra but got no reply. He went back to the kitchen.

He noticed the drawer he had opened earlier to get the first aid kit was pulled out a few inches. He had closed it completely. He pulled it open wider and a frown creased his brow. What else had been inside it?

Before he could remember, the back door burst open—the same one he had shattered earlier—and Kendra staggered inside. She turned off the flashlight that he belatedly remembered seeing in the drawer. She stopped short at sight of him.

"So you're still here?" she said in a strange voice.

"Of course I'm still here. What are you doing out of bed?"

"I remembered that I forgot to take care of the dogs. Jenna couldn't get here and I had to do it." She closed her eyes and leaned weakly against the counter as she dropped the flashlight back into the drawer.

"Kendra, you need to get back into bed." Jared touched her arm and found her shivering. "Now you seem to be having a chill."

"Is that part of the poisoning?"

"No. I called Dr. Phillips. Chills and fever are not part of the process." He turned her to face him, reached up to smooth his thumb over her silken eyebrows. "And if you were still suffering from the original poisoning, your eyebrows would have started to fall out by now. Dr. Phillips is pretty sure you just have a virus. If I have any reason to suspect otherwise, Mark and Phil are on stand-by to come and get you at first light."

She remained listlessly by the counter, as if she could barely support her own weight. Her lids drooped.

"What dogs?" Jared asked, as her earlier explanation finally registered.

"The companion dogs."

"The what?"

"The dogs that I own. The dogs that I train."

Jared stared at her. "Kendra, what is this place? Where is this place?"

"Canine Companions is located in northwestern Nevada. We raise and train working and companion dogs. My partner, Tim, is a veterinary student and his friend, Jenna, is a trainer. They take care of things when I'm not around. Abel and Molly Woods live here and oversee things. Except Molly fell a couple of days ago and Abel took her to the doctor and they haven't been able to get back because a tree fell and blocked the road."

She looked at Jared still watching her silently and licked her dry lips.

"And since I can't cook, I've been slowly starving to death because I couldn't get into town for food. And then I wasn't hungry and I was too tired to care. Can I have more juice now, please?"

"Kendra," Jared said on a ragged sigh as he dragged her into his arms and cradled her shivering body close to his warmth. He managed to take down a glass and fill it with juice while still holding her. "What am I going to do with you?" he asked as he released her enough to hand her the glass.

Kendra took the glass and sipped the cool juice, savoring the feel of it against her scratchy throat.

"That's not the question," she said, turning to put the glass in the sink. "You still haven't told me how you got here, or why? Matt didn't bring you," she added with certainty.

"How can you be so sure? Did you tell him not to tell me where you were? Didn't that put him in the unappealing position of taking sides against friends?"

"No, but he would have called to tell me you were coming."

"Matt wasn't at Holland. He had just left to take Kris to the hospital to have the baby. Bret figured out the GPS coordinates where Matt had dropped you off and brought me to the same spot."

"I must be getting careless if it was that easy to find me." She moved toward the door. "I'm going to bed now. When I wake up you will be gone and I will know that I only imagined you here."

"Kendra," Jared waited until she reached the door before he spoke. She turned back to look at him. "Why would you imagine me here?"

Confusion clouded her eyes. She wet her lips. "I just—I thought—"

"Could it maybe be because you would like me to be here with you? That you want that as much as I do." He didn't have to try and make his voice low and persuasive. The husky tones were real enough. Suddenly her answer was all important.

She caught her bottom lip between her teeth for a moment as she considered. "There's nothing I want more than to have you with me always," she said. "Even thought we have only had a few minutes together when we weren't fighting for our lives or dodging danger, as it were, I know that you are the only man I've ever wanted to be with. I'm just—" she broke off.

"Yes?" Jared prompted when she did not continue.

"—not sure it would work." She shrugged. "Being the people we are, can we live without the element of danger? Would we be happy?"

"You're forgetting that I've been retired for several years, until I met you and sorta stepped back into the danger zone."

"But I'm not forgetting how bored you were, even with Double E. I wouldn't like knowing I was responsible for that."

He held her gaze. "Do you think I could be bored with you around?"

"I don't think I have the courage to find out. I don't have dreams anymore—at least not ones that involve other people. I just—exist. It's safer that way." She turned away again. "In case you are real," she said over her shoulder, "you can sleep in Tim's room upstairs. If you need clean sheets, they should be in the closet." She made her way down the hall to her room.

Jared stared after her, feeling the world crashing around him.

Lose…lose…lose…

CHAPTER SEVENTEEN

Jared returned the saw to the back of the truck and dragged a heavy chain over to the tree that still blocked the road. After working about an hour he finally had it in several chunks small enough to deal with. When he first arrived at the scene, he had been amazed at the amount of work Kendra had accomplished, especially as sick as she appeared to be.

He had left her sleeping peacefully, her temperature back to normal. He found the kennels and again registered surprise at the extent of the operation she had going here. He fed and watered the dogs, all strong and beautiful with bright intelligent eyes. As he watched them eating his mind flashed to another group of dogs, also strong, beautiful and intelligent, but a bit larger and more aggressive. What would Kendra think of his guard and security dog program? He had just received an offer from the military that would enable him to focus completely on that as a career.

Startled out of his thoughts, he had grabbed a ringing phone inside the kennel, answering instinctively.

"Jared Hall."

A long pause.

"*Major* Jared Hall?"

Jared sighed, long and audibly. "That would be me."

"I'm sorry, sir. You don't know me but you've been my hero ever since you rescued Kendra in Kuwait. My name is Tim Matthews. I work with Kendra. I wondered if the tree is still blocking the road."

"I think it may be. Kendra said something about someone not being able to get here because a tree had fallen and blocked the road."

"I'm supposed to come out today, but I need to know if I'm going to be able to get through."

"Why don't you call back in about an hour? I'll go check out the tree and see what I can do."

Now Jared looked down at the tree at his feet. All he had to do was drag the pieces of the trunk to the side of the road and just about any vehicle should be able to get through. He heard the sound of an engine approaching and looked up as a shiny black truck came to a stop on the other side of the fallen tree.

A young man jumped out of the truck and came forward.

"Hello, Major. I'm Tim. I thought I might as well come on out. Either the road would be clear or I figured I could help."

Jared shook the hand Tim offered. "Please. Call me Jared. I'm just getting ready to try and pull these pieces out of the road. You can secure the chain and I'll see what I can do about dragging them to the side."

Working together, it took another twenty minutes to clear the road enough to get Tim's truck through. Jared threw the chain into the old truck he was driving and followed the shiny black vehicle back to the kennels.

"Where's Kendra?" Tim asked as they started toward the house. "I've never known her to sleep in."

"She wasn't feeling well last night when I got here. I think she must have picked up a virus."

Kendra watched from the window as Jared and Tim walked up from the kennels. She had showered and dressed in jeans and a flannel shirt over a T-shirt. She felt weak and a little light headed, but not nearly as achy and feverish as the night before.

So she hadn't imagined Jared? She still wasn't clear how he had gotten here, or how she felt about his presence. She drank in his lithe stride and strong fit body as he easily kept pace with the younger man.

Dear God, what am I supposed to do now? You aren't supposed to tempt me beyond my ability to resist, and I'm not sure there's a woman alive who could resist Jared Hall.

Jared glanced up from preparing breakfast to see Kendra standing in the doorway. She looked as weak as a kitten but was putting up a brave front. He reached for a glass and opened the refrigerator to fill it with juice.

"Good morning. Breakfast will be ready in a few minutes. You can drink this while you wait." He put the glass on the bar and watched as she crossed the room to sit down. "Are you feeling better? Any more hallucinations?"

She reached for the glass and a corner of her mouth quirked up. "That still depends on whether or not you are real. Where's Tim? I saw him walking with you."

"Getting something from his truck. He's been telling me about your operation here. You've put a lot into it." *Should he tell her about his dogs?*

"Define a lot."

"Time. Money. Effort."

She shrugged. "Actually, this place belonged to my grandparents. My parents weren't interested in it so I paid all the back taxes and got everything repaired. The only other real expense was the two shepherds. They've done all the work."

"Looks like you have about a dozen dogs ready to train and a half dozen coming along."

"And Connie is ready to deliver any day now."

"I guess I didn't see her when I fed the dogs this morning."

"That's because Tim took her to his clinic so he could keep an eye on her. We didn't know when I would be here."

"Speaking of that," Jared glanced around. "Do you have a radio or television? Anyway we can get any news of the rest of the world?"

Kendra walked over to a cabinet and slid a rollup door aside to reveal a built-in television. She picked up the remote and walked back to the bar.

"I'm almost afraid—" She broke off as the television powered up and she flipped through the channels to a twenty-four hour news network.

A timer went off and Jared turned back to the oven where he removed a cookie sheet containing his famous "oven" pancake. The wonderful aroma wafting from it drew Kendra's attention and she felt her mouth water.

"That smells heavenly," she sighed. "What do I have to do to get some of it? Name your price."

"When I told you breakfast would be ready in a few minutes, didn't that imply an invitation?" Jared asked as he put the pan on the counter to cool.

"Sometimes you can get into trouble if you assume things."

Jared stopped to look at her. "I thought we had moved beyond that," he said, holding her gaze.

Kendra looked away. Then her head jerked up and she sucked in her breath. Jared turned to see her gaze riveted to the television. The sound was muted but she was reading the ticker along the bottom of the screen.

"Turn on the sound," Jared said, his voice tense.

Kendra picked up the remote with trembling hands. After a moment, Jared took it from her and turned off the *Mute* function.

"*...Region One power grid which includes all the Northeastern United States. The explosion that occurred was in a reactor that was mothballed earlier this year. The Eastern seaboard is on Red Alert. Repeat, the security alert has been increased to Red...*"

"I failed!" Kendra whispered, her face void of color. "Dear God, I failed." She put her hands over her face.

Jared reached for her and caught her as she might have slipped off the stool. He gathered her close, his eyes still on the screen before him.

"*I repeat,*" the reporter was saying, "*several threats were received this morning to power plants and nuclear reactors within the Region One power grid. A small explosion has occurred within an older mothballed reactor. No sign of radioactivity as yet. Security Alert Red.*"

"What's this all about, Kendra?" Jared asked. "Is this related to your last assignment?"

Kendra straightened and visibly pulled herself together. "We figured that the target was the Region One power grid with the intention of shutting down all the nuclear reactors. At that point we figured there would be explosions, contaminating the entire eastern United States with radioactive fallout. We traced all the missing plutonium I had been tracking to domestic sites. It never left the country. The locket didn't just contain a transmitter. It had a microchip that contained all this information. They used me to transfer information to colleagues in this country. That's why they had to get the locket back. When the locket was *returned* to them, the microchip had been replaced with a similar one with slightly altered information. We had operatives in place everywhere. I don't know what could have gone wrong." She sank back on the bar stool. "I failed—"

Jared caught her shoulders. "Kendra, *no*. Didn't you hear what they said? There have been threats received, but only one small explosion that produced no radiation. General Starr is on top of it. They have to make them think they're succeeding in order to lure them into the trap."

Kendra stared at him, unconvinced. She turned back to the television. "I have to call the general—"

"No, Kendra. He has his hands full right now. You're job is done. He knows that. He said as much when he told me how to find you.

"But what if I failed?" Her lips trembled and her eyes swam with unshed tears.

"You didn't fail," Jared said. "My money is on you, Kendra."

"My little brother used to say that," Kendra said, her voice so dry it cracked. "I failed him."

Before Jared could think of a reply, Tim burst through the back door, pausing when it wobbled on its hinges.

184

"What happened here?" he asked with a frown.

Jared glanced at him. "That's a long story. I'll fix it after breakfast." He glanced at the stove. "Speaking of which, it should be cool enough to eat about now."

He proceeded to cut the pancake into portions and dish it onto plates which he handed to Tim and Kendra. He put butter and maple syrup on the counter, refilled his coffee and straddled a stool.

"Eat up. Kendra, I hope you finally have an appetite." He caught her gaze and quirked a brow to try and convey the need for normalcy.

She looked at him for a moment, toying with her fork. Then a faint smile touched her lips, although it did not dispel the shadows in her eyes.

"I believe I do," she agreed.

"I came in with good news," Tim said. "I clean forgot it when I saw that door." He frowned again as he looked at it.

"We could use some good news about now," Kendra agreed.

"How about this? Connie has eight healthy puppies. Rusty and I delivered them this morning. Five females and three males. Just the mix we were hoping for."

"Wow!" Kendra's eyes sparkled. "I'm going to have to get some of these guys out of here to their new homes soon, before those get too big and I run out of space."

"I took a look at your dogs this morning," Jared said. "I'm impressed. Do you already have some of them placed?" He asked to keep Kendra distracted.

"All but three. And the others, the ones with homes to go to, are ninety-nine percent trained already. Jenna is a wonder."

"Jenna is good, but you already had them well on their way," Tim said loyally. "You made her job easy."

Kendra frowned. "But without her, they would have forgotten everything I taught them."

"Well, I still say, without you, this operation wouldn't be half what it is. Are we ever going to get you here full time?"

"Well, it's good to hear that I'm wanted," Kendra hedged, "but as far as I'm concerned, you and Jenna contribute just as much as I do." Another frown. "Are you two fighting again—or something?"

A corner of Tim's mouth twitched. "I'll go for the 'or something' defense." Then, "Hey, Jared, this is really great. You need to teach Kendra to make it. That way, maybe she won't starve to death if we're not around."

Kendra snorted. "Better men than Jared have tried to teach me to cook. You know how hopeless I am." She got up to carry her plate to the sink.

"Yes, but I really don't think I'm the better man," Tim said, twisting her words, his grin unrepentant. "I don't know how any woman can be so good at everything else, and so inept in the kitchen."

"Hey, watch it!" Kendra said with mock ferocity. "While you stay home and deliver puppies, I could be out saving the world for humanity for all you know. Give me a break."

"Speaking of that," Tim said, his attention suddenly turned to the television. "What's happening on the east coat?"

CHAPTER EIGHTEEN

Jared heard Kendra's intake of breath, looked up to see her staring at Tim in horror. He put a hand on her shoulder, gently easing her back down on the barstool.

"We just caught an update, but haven't heard any real details," he said, his voice and pose casual. "What do you know about it?"

Tim swallowed a bite of pancake. "It broke while we were delivering the puppies, so I didn't catch everything. It seems there were fluctuations in the power grid this morning in a couple of northeastern states—Massachusetts and Jersey, I believe. Then all the nuc plants started getting threats. The one explosion, they aren't even sure it's related. That plant was mothballed several months ago."

"What kind of threats?" Jared asked. He felt Kendra relax and withdrew his hand. "Do they want money? Prisoners released? Any idea who is behind the threats?"

"You'd make a great interrogator," Tim commented. He drained his coffee and got up to refill the mug. "Apparently they haven't made any demands. Just weird sayings like *'Today is the beginning of the end...'* and *'This is the first day of the last days of your life'*. Kinda spooky."

"Do cell phones work out here?" Jared asked. "I have a friend I can call who might know something."

"Cell service is very erratic. Best to use the land line." Tim went back to drop down on his stool. "This looks new," he said as he again focused on the television.

Jared and Kendra turned as one to watch the incoming newscast. At sight of the mushrooming black smoke in the photo behind the reporter, Kendra again sucked in her breath.

"Dear God..." she whispered.

"As bad as it looks," the newscaster read dutifully from his teleprompter, *"we continue to be reassured that this is not a nuclear explosion. No radiation has been detected. Helicopters flying over say the fire appears to have originated in a storage area of the facility."*

Kendra whirled to stare at Jared. "I have to make a phone call," she said. "Maybe the explosion wasn't supposed to spread radiation—" She rushed from the room.

Total silence fell over the table and Jared raised his head to look at Tim.

"She wasn't kidding, was she?" Tim asked rhetorically. "When she said that part about *'saving the world for humanity'*."

And although he knew the question was only rhetorical, Jared still felt compelled to answer.

"No. She wasn't kidding." He stood and carried his dishes to the sink.

"Sir, I know this isn't a good time to call, but I've thought of something." Kendra drummed her fingers on the desk.

"Agent Allen," the familiar growl felt somehow reassuring. "We're on top of this, I assure you."

"But sir, I still haven't figured out the thallium angle. What if the explosions aren't meant to spread radiation, but some biological or chemical agent, probably with similar symptoms to thallium poisoning. That way when my symptoms, and Major Hall's symptoms, started to show up, they would be just like those experienced by everyone else."

Total silence followed. After a few seconds, Kendra spoke again, her voice slightly breathless. "Sir, are you still there? I—"

"I'm here, Agent. Give me a moment to ask a couple of questions. I'll get back to you." A click followed by depressingly soothing elevator music filled her ear as General Starr put her on hold.

"You put me on hold! How dare—"

She whirled as the receiver was removed from her fingers as she began beating it against the desk. Jared drew her close.

"Kendra, love, you have to let the general do his job. Trust me, they have every angle covered."

"How can you be sure? This is too important—"

"Remember when we argued about the definition of trust?" Jared asked, seeking and holding her gaze..

189

"When I said that I had confidence in my fellow operatives based on previous experience. That I *knew* they would do their jobs." She dropped her gaze. "The problem is that none of us have this kind of previous experience."

"Hello, is anyone there?"

Jared put the receiver to his ear. "Major Hall speaking, sir."

"Major," the General sounded pleased. "I see you found her. Try and keep her distracted. We're on top of this."

"Maybe you should tell her that, sir." He handed the phone to Kendra and stepped away from her.

He was aware of the quiet murmur of Kendra's voice as he walked over to glance out the window. A white sport utility vehicle pulled into the drive and a man got out and went over to help a woman who was struggling with crutches.

"I have a message from the general," Kendra said behind him. She peered over his shoulder. "Oh, good! Abel and Molly are back." She drew in her breath. "But she's on crutches. That can't be good."

Jared turned. "What message?"

She looked at him. "Message? Oh, he said to consider that an order."

"Consider what an order?" Jared asked.

"How would I know?" She sounded a little miffed. "Whatever he said to you just now."

The brief conversation flashed through Jared's mind. There was only one part of it that could be considered an order. His eyes flashed and a corner of his mouth tilted in a grin.

"Aye, aye, sir. Whatever you say, sir." He reached for Kendra and pulled her into his arms.

190

"What are you doing?" she asked, peering at him through her lashes.

"Following orders." His arms tightened as he gathered her close.

"I don't understand." Her voice sounded breathless and a little uncertain.

"You don't have to. We're on top of this." He lowered his head and covered her lips with his.

"Jared—"

"Yes, love."

"You're trying to distract me."

He grinned. "Is it working?"

She stared at him for a moment, then reached up and pulled his face down to hers. "Try harder," she whispered, her voice husky.

Jared forced himself to break the kiss that Kendra had initiated but in which he had been more than a willing participant. He gathered Kendra close and rested his chin against her hair, breathing in her clean fragrance. Her hair was still slightly damp and smelled of herbal shampoo.

He forced himself to try and identify the scent as he struggled for the control that having Kendra in his arms had so sorely compromised.

"I didn't realize following the general's orders meant hazardous duty," Jared said as he finally put Kendra away to hold her at arms length.

"Hazardous duty?" Her voice came out a surprised squeak.

He reached out to trace a knuckle down her cheek. "You pack a lethal punch, little one."

Kendra swallowed. "You should talk." She searched his face for a long moment. "Jared, you still haven't told me why you're here. Last night I kept thinking I was imagining you. But not even my imagination could come up with a kiss like that."

"Lavender," he said. "And something else—a touch of mint."

"Wintergreen." Her nose scrunched. "And you reek slightly of sweat, leather, and pine. I'm guessing you must have removed the tree so that Tim and Abel could get through."

"Actually, Tim showed up in time to help me." He watched her carefully. "He didn't know, did he? About your job—what you do—until just now."

"I never told him, but he's always been a pretty sharp kid. I did tell him about you rescuing me in Kuwait. He may have figured out what that meant."

"He did seem to recognize my name," Jared said dryly. He turned away. "Who is he, Kendra? Why does the name sound so familiar?"

She stared at him, wet her lips. "Tim—Timmy Matthews—the little boy who was there when Bobby—when—"

Jared turned back to see her trembling. She put a hand to her mouth.

"How could I have forgotten?" Jared whispered. "Kendra, I'm so sorry." He put his hands on her arms. "So you have stayed in touch with him all these years?"

She laughed, a dry, brittle sound. "*Stayed in touch*. We've been virtually inseparable. When two people share the same living nightmare as long as we have—I, well, we sort of watch out for each other. He worries about me. I keep an eye on him. He seems to have turned out pretty well. The only thing that concerns me is his relationship with Jenna. I think she cares for him, but he doesn't treat her very well."

"What about his parents?" Jared asked.

"What about them?"

"Were they able to move on from that night, put it behind them?"

She shrugged. "As well as any of us have, I suppose." She turned away. "I need to go check on Molly—see if she needs any help." She paused at the door. "By the way, thanks for the distraction!" She blew him a kiss and disappeared down the hall.

A wry grin twisted Jared's mouth. "Anytime, my love!" He sat down at her desk and reached for the phone.

Kendra found Molly and Abel in the den watching the newscaster on the widescreen. Tim had joined them.

"Anything new?" Kendra asked from the doorway.

Tim looked at her. Shrugged. "Sounds like it's about over. They've arrested dozens of people, everyone is standing down, and the alert has been downgraded." He stood up. "I think I'll go visit the dogs." As he passed Kendra, he punched her lightly on the arm. "Good work, kid!" he said under his breath.

She stared after him, until she became aware that Molly had spoken to her. She turned.

"I'm sorry. Did you say something?"

Molly smiled. "Just that I'm sorry I wasn't here when you arrived. Did you manage to handle everything all right?"

Kendra shrugged. "I survived—with a little help from a friend. Actually, I need to talk to you about a room for him. Last night I let him use Tim's room."

"I won't be much help, but if you feel up to cleaning up the attic room, he's welcome to that. Otherwise, he could use the daybed in here."

"I guess I need to find out how long he plans to stay," Kendra said. "I'm going to clean up the kitchen."

CHAPTER NINETEEN

Jared found Kendra in the kitchen a few minutes later. He watched for a moment as she stood at the sink, staring out the window. He walked over to her, touched her arm.

"It's over, love. The good guys came through, thanks to you."

She turned to look at him, her face wet with the tears that streamed silently down her face.

Jared stared at her. "You saved us again, Kendra. Why are you crying?" He brushed the tears off her cheeks.

"It doesn't seem fair, somehow," she said. She drew a sobbing breath. "I can save hundreds, maybe even thousands of lives, but I couldn't save one small boy. Why did Bobby have to die?"

Jared drew her into his arms and pressed her face against his shoulder. He buried his face in her hair and closed his eyes.

God, help me find the words. Michael said I needed to ask You for help in this. I know this is way too critical for me to handle alone.

"Let's go outside," Jared said, feeling the walls close in on him. He took Kendra's hand and led her out through the broken door to the back porch. He dropped down into a glider and pulled her down beside him, putting an arm around her shoulders.

"Kendra, are you a Christian?" he asked, not knowing quite where else to start and suddenly needing to know.

He felt her shrug. "I was. I haven't prayed much—since Bobby. There didn't seem to be much point."

"Neither have I, until lately. I'll tell you about that later. But you have become someone I don't think I can go on without. You have to come to terms with what happened all those years ago."

"Oh, sure—" She pulled away from him and tried to stand. He caught her hand and pulled her back down.

"Kendra, do you think you would have done what you've done— chosen the career you chose—if you hadn't lost Bobby."

"Of course not. I chose the most potentially self-destructive route I could find. Not consciously, I realize now, but that *is* what I did. I didn't want to live. I would do anything, go anywhere."

"And that made you an invaluable tool to the DIA, did it not?"

"They seemed to think so."

"And what just happened—the intelligence you gathered, you're ability to interpret it, and your determination to follow the mission through. Don't you think that might have been God's plan all along? You were where you needed to be—when He needed you there. And without Bobby's death, you would never have taken that step."

She stared at her hands. "How can you even began to understand? Have you ever lost anyone—"

"Yes."

Kendra froze then raised her head to look at him. "Tell me, please. I need to understand you. Why you are so afraid to become involved with me."

Jared sighed and stretched out his legs. "I had a high school sweetheart," he said, his voice wooden. His mouth twisted. "Amanda thought I was bigger than life. That I was braver, smarter, and stronger than anyone else in the world."

Kendra threw him a glance, looked away. She crossed her arms over her chest. "Sounds like she was right on target so far."

She felt Jared's glance. He cleared his throat. "Yeah, well, she also thought I would always be there to take care of her. To protect her."

Kendra jumped up before Jared could stop her. "I don't know if I want to hear this. I'm not sure—"

"Sit down, Kendra. You have to hear this if you want to understand."

She sank down on a bench across from him, arms still forming a protective barrier.

"I didn't know what I wanted to do with my life," Jared went on after a moment. "I knew I wasn't ready to settle down. So I joined the army and found my niche. I went into Special Forces and became a team leader." He paused to organize his thoughts. "Then while I was in Kuwait—"

"Rescuing me," Kendra said dryly.

"Among other things. Anyway, no one really knows what happened, but they found her body in the river. It didn't appear to be suicide. She wasn't much of a swimmer. She was afraid of the water and I didn't insist she learn to swim."

"I'm so sorry," Kendra whispered, her voice choked.

"Maybe that's why I pushed you so hard about your fears," Jared continued after a moment. "Then, when push came to shove, I found out you were better at protecting yourself—and me—than I was. That was a bit of a blow to my over-inflated ego."

Jared stood and paced restlessly for a few seconds. "At first, I couldn't handle the fact that I had put you in danger, after I had insisted you had to have complete trust in me. All I could think of was how I had let Amanda down. But somewhere along the line, I began to realize that you could take care of yourself. You didn't need me for that."

"But I did need you." Kendra caught his hand and pulled him down to sit beside her on the bench. "When I showed up at your cabin just as it blew up—well, I had every intention of getting some answers. But you weren't in any condition to talk, and I realized our friends on the other side intended to play for keeps. I got side-tracked for a while there. And then, I wasn't sure any of us had a future."

Jared turned his hand until it closed around hers and squeezed gently..

"Tell me about Amanda," Kendra said. "What did she look like?"

"She was small and blonde. Delicate. Almost ethereal. The kind of woman that brought out all the protective instincts in a man."

"Of course," Kendra agreed, her voice flat.

Jared frowned and looked at her. "What does that mean?"

"I suppose she had cornflower blue eyes, too."

"No. Actually, they were green."

"She sounds like my friend, Kris Holland. Walker now. Matt's wife."

"Kris is nothing like Amanda. Kris is incredibly strong, emotionally and physically. Amanda was neither of those things."

"That's the kind of woman I can see you being attracted to. You were her hero."

"Again, meaning what?" Jared growled.

"That tall dark Amazon types don't attract strong men. And there isn't any other kind that we would want." She tried to stand but Jared still held her hand and showed no intention of freeing it.

Jared turned to her. "Is it so impossible for you to believe that I've grown up a bit since Amanda? That maybe my preferences for women have changed as well?"

Kendra shook her head. "Jared, I feel something for you that I've never felt for anyone else. But you see what a basket case I am. How can you possibly want to have anything to do with me?"

Jared touched her mouth, gently drew the pad of his thumb across her bottom lip, trailed his knuckle down her cheek.

"Because I think this is what God wants me to do at this point in my life. This is where He wants me to be. I have to be here for you—help you heal if that is possible."

Both Jared and Kendra tensed as the sound of a powerful engine rose up from the valley below.

"That will be Matt—or Bret—with your parents," Jared said casually.

"My parents!" Kendra stared at him.

Jared shrugged. "I was getting around to preparing you, but I got sidetracked talking about Amanda. I called them last night. There is something they have to tell you. Something you should have been told twelve years ago, but they couldn't bring themselves to. It is something your father mentioned and I think you need to hear it." He stood. "I will be going back on the plane. I'll take the truck down to meet them. You can go or not. Just be here when they get back."

Jared took a deep breath and looked at Kendra. The stricken look on her face was almost his undoing.

"I'm sorry, but I had to do this. What your parents will tell you should make a major difference in how you view what happened. If it doesn't, then I guess this is good-by. If it does, your father will know where you can find me." He crossed the porch and pushed open the door. "I'm sorry I don't have time to fix the door. I promised…"

"I'll take care of it." Tim said from behind them.

Jared turned to face him, a brow quirked in question.

Tim shrugged. "You're right. She has to hear this—and from her parents. They told me a few years ago." He appeared lost in thought for a long moment. "It helped. Of course I had to verify it, make sure it wasn't something they came up with to make me feel better."

Tim turned to Kendra. "Go with Jared. Bring your parents back. I'll be here for you." He looked at Jared and held out his hand. "Thank you for doing this. We'll get her straightened out and let her know where to find you."

Jared clasped the younger man's hand. "Thank you for standing by her all these years. Hopefully—I can take over that job soon."

Tim grinned. "I'll relinquish it with pleasure."

Jared stepped inside to pick up the duffle bag he had never unpacked.

"Matt said to tell you to stop by the house before you leave," Bret Brown said as he shut off the engine. "And to make sure you did, I believe he took the keys to the Jeep."

Jared couldn't help a grin. "Captain Walker always did know how to get what he wanted."

"And sometimes a bit more than he bargained for," Bret said.

"What does that mean?"

"You'll see. I wouldn't want to spoil it for you."

Jared tossed his duffle bag into his Jeep. In case he really wanted to leave without seeing Matt and Kris, he had a spare set of keys, but what harm could there be in humoring Matt?

The door swung open in answer to his knock, and for a moment Jared could only stare. It actually took a few seconds to process that the man standing before him with a towel tied around his waist and another slung over his shoulder, cradling an infant in his arms, was the spit and polish Matthew Walker he had come to know over the years.

Matt grinned. "Jared! I hoped you would stop by."

"Did I have a choice?" Jared stepped inside as Matt held the door open with his free hand. "Who do we have here?" he asked, indicating the baby trying to focus on him with wide open eyes.

"Major, I would like you to meet our son, Joseph Benjamin Holland Walker, who will be known as Joey." Matt performed the formal introductions. "Joey just fell asleep or I would introduce you to him."

"Really? Does he always sleep with his eyes open?" Jared pushed the blanket aside for a better look.

Matt looked down. "Well, I'll be—! I guess I still have a lot to learn. Since he stopped screaming, I thought he had fallen asleep. Well, then, Joey, meet Major Jared Hall. I'm sure—"

"My son does not scream," a voice said behind Jared. "He just happens to have very healthy lungs. Hello, Jared."

He turned and for the second time in as many minutes, Jared could only stare. Kris Holland had always been one of the most beautiful women he had ever met, but now, standing before him, cradling an infant— He looked back at Matt.

Cradling an infant?

"Hey, wait! What is this?" He glanced again from Matt to Kris and back again. *"Twins?"*

"We had no idea," Kris grinned. "I should have picked up on some of the obvious signs, but I told my doctor not to tell me anything, other than that the baby was healthy. So we were a wee bit surprised."

"So who is this?" Again Jared reached out and this time a tiny fist wrapped around his finger.

"Oh, my, flirting already, are we, Jeana? Not that I question your tastes." Kris smiled at Jared. "This is our daughter, Jeana Elizabeth Walker. Now, she does scream—"

As if to underscore her mother's words, baby Jeana let loose with an ear piercing wail. Jared winced.

"Sorry about that," Kris said as she placed the baby over her shoulder, gently patting her back. "Will you stay for dinner, Jared? I need to hear about Kendra."

"How can I refuse? I need to talk about Kendra."

A few hours later Jared turned to take a last look at the couple before him, each cradling a baby in one arm. Matt and Kris made the absolute picture of domestic bliss, and as well as he knew them, he knew that this was for real. Not that anyone deserved to be happy more than these two, he admitted. They had been through a lot on their way to where they were now. He gave a final wave and went down the steps. He heard the door close behind him.

He just hoped there would be enough of this kind of happiness to go around. That there was still some left over for him.

CHAPTER TWENTY

Kendra stared at her parents, her fists knotted at her sides. Her whole body trembled as silent tears streamed down her face. She had tried to prepare herself for this confrontation, putting it off as long as possible as she prepared the attic room for guests. She couldn't imagine what they might have to tell her after all these years and how they could possibly believe it might make a difference. And now, the reality was horrifying.

"You're telling me that Bobby would have died anyway. That he was ill. Why didn't I know this?" Her always husky voice came out a strained croak.

"There was one final round of tests we were waiting for before we told you. You might remember that Bobby missed a lot of school that semester. He always seemed to have a cold. We didn't want to tell you until we had all the facts and the results of those last tests didn't come back until after—" Jim Allen paused to clear his throat. His wife clung to his hand as if it were a lifeline.

"Until Bobby was already dead," Kendra's father continued, his voice thick with tears. "But they confirmed our worst fears. He had an acute form of leukemia. We would have been willing to do anything, even bone marrow transplants. We already had ourselves tested and your mother would have been a good match. But the prognosis was not good. Everything we would have done, all the suffering we would have put him through, would only have bought a few months—"

"You don't know that!" Kendra challenged, her eyes sparking angrily, drying away the tears..

Jim shook his head. "No. Not as a certainty. We only had the expert's opinion. But with what happened, after our initial grief and shock, we felt that God in His all knowing wisdom did not want Bobby to suffer any longer. And at that point, we didn't know how to tell you because we were afraid you would react exactly as you're reacting now. *You feel that we wanted him dead. That it was a relief to lose him before we all had to go through the pain of his illness.* We lost you as well, for all intents and purposes. That was the part we couldn't bear. Not only had we lost our precious son, but we lost our wonderful daughter as well.

"We're telling you this now, because we want you back, Kendra. And not only do we want you back, but there's a fine young man out there who has been desperately trying to help you. Are you going to condemn him to the solitary existence he has chosen for so long? Or will you try and believe that what happened to your brother was God's will and purpose for him, and that you were in no way responsible?"

Kendra jogged through the mud and driving rain, oblivious to the discomfort as she tried, not for the first time, to outrun her past. With the sudden storm, it would be another day before a plane from Holland Aviation could arrive to pick up her parents, and perhaps her as well. That was a decision she still had to make. She dropped down on a fallen log, partially sheltered by dense foliage. She loved it here. Or she had until Jared arrived and she realized all the things missing in her life.

She wanted it all, she realized now. She wanted what Matt and Kris had. It had taken a while for them to get together. Matt had battled his own demons since his experiences in Desert Storm. She and Matt had a lot in common. He had lost a childhood friend to a tragic death and a few years later his father had been lost while flying an experimental plane. Matt might be the one person who carried more emotional baggage that she herself, Kendra realized. Yet, Kris, with her love and gentle caring had broken through his wall of protective armor.

Just as Jared had broken through hers, Kendra saw with a flash of insight. Now that she knew about Amanda, she could understand why he had initially been reluctant to get involved with her. She and Amanda had nothing in common other than that Jared cared for them. Jared was as emotionally wounded as she and Matt had been. Fortunately for Matt, he had Kris. Who did she have besides Jared, and who did he have besides her? Was it somehow possible that she could meet him halfway—

Even as the thought formed, Kendra rejected it. No way would Jared ever settle for anything from her that was less than everything she had to give. What did she expect, anyway? It was his all or nothing, take no prisoners attitude that had attracted her to him in the first place.

Kendra looked up to see that the rain has stopped. She stood up to peer through the wet branches and caught her breath. As the sun battled to break through the storm clouds to the west, shards of light pierced the clouds, sending out rays that split the sky into light and dark.

Kendra shivered. *"That is me,"* she whispered. *"I've been caught in the darkness of the storm. Now I've come to the edge. Jared is the light and he is reaching out for me. Do I have the courage to cross the line and step into the sunshine? I've been in the storm for so long..."*

"I know how to take charge and make things happen." Suddenly SueAnn's words echoed through Kendra's mind. What if...? A smile touch her lips as a plan began to form. And if it turned out she needed help putting her plan into action, she knew just where to get it.

Jared straightened from splitting rails and wiped sweat off his forehead. The last thing he needed was one last heat wave at the end of September. He was more than ready for cooler weather. He wanted snow, enough to shut him in for weeks. He glared at the sun still halfway to the horizon in the west.

"Snow bound in love... What more could I want... What more could I dream than to be snowbound in love with you."

Of course, he'd hoped Kendra would be here by now. Being snow bound with her would have been his every dream come true. Fat chance of that now. Of course, there didn't seem to be much chance of being snow bound under any conditions. He wiped his brow again and picked up his ax.

The next move was up to her. That's the way he'd left it. He raised the ax again and brought in down with jarring force. The rail split cleanly and he tossed the ax aside. He straightened and speared his fingers into his hair.

So where did he get off issuing a 'My way or the highway' ultimatum to the woman he loved? He was doing it for her own good, he argued to himself. She didn't have to be perfect for him to love her. She just had to at least like herself again. She had to want to live. If she couldn't do those things, how could she love him back?

Jared dropped down on the hillside and stared out over the valley where he had grown up. Scenes flashed through his mind and he felt Kendra in his arms again, felt her lips move under his. This time he let the memories come, too exhausted to fight them. He remembered her strength and her endearing helplessness as she tried to talk to him around the thermometer in her mouth. Most of all, he remembered the look of betrayal as he climbed aboard the Cessna with Bret. He had turned back to hold her for a moment, felt her tremble. It had taken all his strength to leave her.

For the past two weeks, he had fixed up a vacant cabin on the property and built kennels. Phil brought over his two favorite dogs from the breeding program they had started a few years earlier. Their search and guard dogs had attracted the attention of the military as well as police and fire departments all over. He hadn't had a chance to tell Kendra about his breeding program. What would she think of what he was doing? She could easily continue training her dogs along side his somewhat larger and more aggressive charges. Funny that they had both gravitated to dogs for their future fulfillment. As opposed to people, for instance.

Speaking of which, Jared's attention was caught by two streaks of black and brown racing toward him across the valley. He frowned. How had the dogs gotten loose? He stood and raised a hand to shade his eyes against the sun. They seemed to be trailing something and after a moment he realized they had picked up his scent. Their baying echoed up from the valley.

Curious as to what would make them go against all their training, he started down the hill to meet them. The dogs arrived just as he reached the valley floor.

"Sultan, what's going on, fellow?" He reached a hand out to the dog, only to jerk it back when he was met with a rumbling growl and bared fangs. He took a step back and tripped over the smaller female, Sheba. Trapped, he looked up at the two dogs standing guard over him. *Holding him prisoner, actually.* He had trained them. He knew better than to move a muscle.

Jared carefully cleared his throat. "Very impressive, guys. You've learned your lessons well. But what's this all about?"

He was vaguely aware of a vehicle approaching, but didn't dare move enough to turn around and see what or who had arrived. He heard footsteps and looked up into Kendra's amused gray eyes.

"Major," she greeted.

He felt his heart leap, but carefully managed to keep a straight face as he glared up at her.

"Care to call your dogs off?" he asked.

"My dogs?"

The merest of shrugs brought a low rumble from Sultan. "If they are willing to change loyalties so quickly, you can have them."

"I wouldn't say they changed loyalties all that quickly," Kendra said, sitting cross-legged on the ground. She plucked a straw and stuck it in her mouth. "When did you retire them?"

"About a year ago, I guess."

"Then I might have been the last person to work with them. I'm a little amazed that they remembered."

Jared swallowed. "Small world, as they say."

"Isn't it?" Kendra studied him for a moment.

"Would you care to call them off?" Jared asked again. "This isn't exactly comfortable."

"I wouldn't think it is. I need to ask you a couple of questions. If you get the answers right, I'll call them off."

"And if I don't?"

"Oh, I'm sure you will be able to sweet talk them into letting you go, sooner or later."

"And if I don't?"

"That will no longer be my problem."

After a moment he nodded. "Ask."

"How long before we can get married?"

"Say what? I—"

"That's not the right answer—"

As if to underscore her words, Sultan growled again. Louder this time.

"All right! Okay—about six hours, I guess."

"Explain."

"If we flew to Vegas. It might take longer. I don't know when there's a flight—"

Kendra glanced at her watch. "In about ten minutes, or as long as it will take you to pack." She stood up, clapped her hands. "Stand down!"

The two dogs immediately relaxed, flopping down on their bellies, tongues wagging.

Jared stared at them. "Oh, no you don't! It will take a lot more than that—"

Kendra held out a hand to help him up. He looked up at her. "Did I just agree to marry you?"

"'fraid so, Major."

Jared took her hand, gave her arm a twist and rolled over to cover her body with his as she tumbled to the ground. Before she could protest, his mouth covered hers. She yielded immediately, raising her arms to circle his

210

neck and draw him closer. Her lips parted and a low moan of pleasure came from deep in her throat.

Finally Jared broke the kiss and raised his head, staring down into her eyes. "Nothing would please me more than to fly to Vegas with you tonight, but won't your parents want a big wedding, white dress and your father walking you down the aisle?"

"They understand that I'm not really into that. They said to do whatever I had to do. So did General Starr. By the way, in case it matters, I'm retired now."

"Thank God," Jared breathed. Then, "So I'm on my own now?"

"On your own?"

"I'm the only one who can keep you out of trouble, keep you on the straight and narrow. That might be more than I bargained for."

Kendra lowered her lashes demurely. "I promise to be good," she whispered.

"How good?" Jared quirked a brow.

"As good as you want me to be."

"That good, huh?" Jared got to his feet and reached down to pull her up beside him. "In case it matters," he said, cradling her close in his arms, "I love you."

Kendra caught her breath. "I had already figured that out, but, yes, it's nice to hear the words."

Jared took her hand as they walked toward his Jeep. He stopped and leaned against the vehicle, holding both her hands in his. "Yes, it would be nice to hear the words."

Kendra reached up to trace a finger tip around his mouth. "I love you,

Major." She stood on tiptoe to give him a lingering kiss. "I've been in love with you since Kuwait."

"Kendra." He waited until her gaze locked with his, squeezed her hands. "My name is not 'Major'."

"Jared." She rested her head against his chest. "It's just that when all I had were fantasies and I never knew if I would see you again, I thought of you as *my Major*. Even Kris referred to you as *my Major* after I told her about you. You didn't know it, but I've been yours since that night in Kuwait."

He stroked her back, not trusting himself to kiss her again. "I, too, have a confession to make," he admitted.

She raised a brow.

"I've always had this weakness for Amazon warriors. After the rescue in Kuwait, I would have this dream where I would be fighting side by side with this beautiful warrior princess, but I could never see her face. I think that was because the face I wanted to see there, I thought belonged to the young man we had rescued. When you told me what happened, everything became clear." He bent to kiss her gently. "Your message got through," he whispered.

She blinked but not before he saw the sheen of tears. "I suspected that you were a closet romantic," she said, giving him a quick peck on the cheek.

"Is that it? Is that the best you can do?" He asked with mock indignation, intending to lighten the mood..

"I'm sure I can do a lot better, but we are on a rather tight schedule."

"We are?"

She opened the door and pushed him into the Jeep. "Mark is standing by with the chopper to fly us to Vegas. We have just enough time to get married and get back here before the front arrives."

"Front? What front?" Jared asked as the dogs jumped into the back of the Jeep.

"The first cold front of the season. Predicted to bring at least a couple of feet of snow to the foothills. I can't think of anything I want to do more than spend our honeymoon snow bound with you."

Jared stared at her in stunned amazement. "And you called me a closet romantic?" Then, "But how did you know--?"

"Snow bound in love... What more could I want... What more could I dream than to be snowbound in love with you." Kendra sang the words, her eyes telling him everything. "When you wouldn't let me listen to that song, I hoped maybe you weren't as indifferent as you wanted me to believe. This is the first chance I've had to follow through on that theory."

Jared laughed, a full joyous sound.

"Bring on Vegas," he grinned. "We'll spend the winter testing your theory—or as long as it takes."

There's only this moment...the past is erased. Just you in my arms for as long as it takes. Snowbound. Snowbound in love...with you...

About the Author

Growing up in a dysfunctional home long before such terminology existed, the author found escape in books. She attributes the wholesome characters created by such authors as Emilie Loring and Grace Livingston Hill with giving direction to her life. After a successful career as a chemist in Houston, today she lives in a private airpark in San Angelo, Texas, with her airline pilot husband of 36 years, two dogs, nine cats, lots of deer and wild turkey—and oh, yes—airplanes!

In the **HEARTland Series**, Eva O'Connor creates the characters for the books *she* wants to read. She strives to keep them wholesome enough for the daughters and granddaughters of all her friends to enjoy as well. If you enjoyed ***ON THE EDGE***, please look for ***BEYOND THE SUNRISE*** coming soon to lulu.com.

www.ingramcontent.com/pod-product-compliance
Lightning Source LLC
Chambersburg PA
CBHW020841260626
47169CB00003B/1079